BALANCING ACT

DONNA KING

KINGFISHER

CHAPTER 1

"Bye, Carli!"

"See you Monday!"

"Miss you already!"

Carli Carroll's friends leaned out of the school bus and waved happily. She walked towards the Jeep belonging to the Triple X Ranch.

"Hey." Her dad's welcome after her trip to gymnastics camp at Breckenridge was brief and to the point, as always. "Throw your bags in the back. Let's get out of here."

"Hi, Dad. Good to see you, Dad. I missed you too, Dad," Carli muttered.

"Yeah, yeah, cut out the clever stuff," Don Carroll replied as he climbed into the cab and turned the ignition. "I got a heap of work to do at the ranch. How about knuckling down and helping, instead of giving me a hard time?"

"Sorry," Carli said, staring ahead as her dad turned the Jeep off the main road and headed along the familiar dirt track towards home. Bump – rattle – roll. Tall redwoods lined the narrow road. Way down below, at the base of the steep, rocky mountainside, the clear green water in Silverfish Creek ran high and fast. "How's Mom?" she asked.

"She's good. Getting ready for a big week next week. Twenty-three guests. This week we have just eighteen."

Rattle – rattle. The Jeep swayed close to the edge of the track. Suddenly a mule deer leapt out of the undergrowth. Carli's dad swerved towards the rockface, then righted the vehicle. "Darn critter," he muttered.

"I got the Best Gymnast award," Carli mentioned at the Five Mile Post. Which, considering she was up against gymnasts from all over Colorado, was a pretty big deal. "By the end of the week I got to work on the hardest moves for my routines."

Don Carroll glanced sideways at his daughter. "Don't go getting ideas," he warned. "Your mom and me can't afford to send you to gymnastics camp all the time as well as paying for your lessons, period."

"I never asked you to."

"Well, don't."

Welcome home, Carli. We're real proud of you. She played a silent game, imagining any normal parent's response. *We always knew you were a born horsewoman, but now it turns out you're an exceptionally talented gymnast too!*

Aw, shucks! she would say modestly in her alternative, apple-pie, rosy-cheeked universe. *It ain't nothing!*

Maybe you're not the sharpest tool in the box, her dad would say with a kindly smile. *But, honey, you sure are the real thing when it comes to sports!*

"I brought in that sorrel two-year-old from Marshy Meadow," her dad told her instead. "I reckon she's ready to sack out."

Carli knew which foal he meant – she'd been there at the birth, when the mare had been in trouble. They'd called in the vet, but the mare had died anyway. Carli had hand-reared the foal, which she'd named Diamond. She also knew her dad's method of schooling the young horse would involve some pretty harsh handling. "I'll do it," she offered quickly.

The Triple X was in sight, nestling in the valley bottom, its pastures strung out beside the creek. Log cabins where the guests stayed were perched on the rocky slopes. The main house stood on the green valley floor.

"OK," Don agreed. "Ben and I will keep an eye on you. Tomorrow's Saturday. Take Diamond into the round pen before breakfast."

"Oh but . . . " Saturday was Carli's gymnastics day when she went into the Springs for training, and he knew it. But she'd been in Breckenridge a whole week. Better not push it. "OK," she agreed. "Tomorrow first thing. I'll be there."

"She's pretty," Lee remarked as Carli worked Diamond in the round pen. "I like the white star on her forehead."

As the newest wrangler on the ranch, Lee had drawn the short straw and had been up since before dawn, bringing horses in from the pastures to saddle them up, ready for dude action. Now he sat on the rail, watching Carli work.

Carli snaked a rope along the ground close behind the young sorrel's back quarters. It sent her forwards at a canter, head up and mane flying in the wind. Diamond kept to the rim of the round pen, keeping ahead of the rope.

"I'm waiting for her head to go down,"

Carli explained. "Then she'll stop running and turn to me. Look, she's doing it now."

Diamond slowed to a trot and lowered her head.

"She's been running a long time. Now she's tired. She's thinking, 'OK, boss, what do you want me to do now?' In other words, she's submitting."

"Neat!" Lee watched closely. "Can I try that?"

"Sure. Send her round anti-clockwise." Carli handed over the rope then hopped up onto the rail. "My dad likes to tie a sack around the hindquarters and make them run. But it scares the heck out of them. I prefer this method."

She glanced at her watch as the wrangler took over. Eight-thirty. She'd skipped breakfast and had been working with Diamond for over an hour, which meant she could finish now and still get to her class in the Springs on time.

"Who's driving into town this

morning?" she asked Lee.

He snaked the rope at Diamond's heels and made her break into a canter around the pen. "Me," he told her. "I need to pick up antibiotics from the vet."

Carli nodded. "Can I hitch a ride?"

"Sure thing." Lee stopped driving Diamond forward the second he saw her lower her head. "Easy, there! Good girl!"

"What time?"

"Nine. I'll finish up here with the colt if you need to get ready."

"Thanks, Lee." Carli grabbed the chance. "Can you put Diamond in with the mares and foals and give her extra grain? I'll meet you in thirty minutes!"

She had thirty minutes to shower and change into clean jeans and T-shirt, to grab her leotard and make herself a quick peanut-butter sandwich to eat during the ride into town.

"How long did you work with the

colt?" her mom asked, coming into the kitchen just as Carli was packing her snack.

Beth Carroll was the same as her husband – short on the hugs and hellos, long on the silences. She was small and thin, with lines on her face that showed she'd lived out in the sun and wind. And she wore the western rig – cowboy boots, jeans and a plaid shirt, with her long, dark hair tied back.

"An hour or more," Carli answered. "She's doing great. Next time I'll do the join-up and try putting a saddle on her."

"Nice work," Beth said quietly. She noticed Carli's gym bag on the kitchen floor and frowned. Carli cringed, waiting for her mother to comment on it. "I was hoping maybe you'd stick around this morning and help with the cabins."

"I'll do it when I get back," Carli promised. "I need to go 'cos I have to tell Lorene about everything that happened while I was away on my gymnastics trip."

Beth went tight-lipped and sniffy. "Life wasn't exactly a breeze round here while you were gone. We were pretty short of help."

How to make a girl feel bad! Her parents could write a book on the subject. "Leave the cabins. I'll do them," she promised again, grabbing her bag before her mom could stop her. "Lee's giving me a ride – he'll be waiting, gotta go!"

Today Lorene, the gymnastics coach, was concentrating on the vault.

"Come off that springboard as if you were launching yourself into outer space!" she told her students. "It has to be explosive from the get-go. Bang – onto the board, and off with all the propulsion you can get!"

Carli was working on her speciality – a piked vault with one and a half twists. The springboard had to launch her onto the table in a handspring, from where she could bound off again in an upwards arc, travelling as far and fast as she could to allow time for the pike and twists.

"You next, Carli!" Lorene yelled. "Stick your landing this time – no extra steps!"

Carli raised herself up to her full height and took a deep breath. She began her run-up with a skip and then a fast sprint. Ahead was the springboard and the table. Beyond that, a soft landing. Lorene stood to one side so she could watch the movement of every muscle in her gymnasts' bodies. She never missed a thing.

Carli's dark, wavy hair was tucked back in a tight ponytail. It bobbed as she sprinted for the board. Bang! Her feet hit the board and she bounced up. She executed a perfect handspring from the table, flying up and folding into piked position, rotating out of it and landing with two feet on the mat. No extra steps, no wobbles.

"Perfect!" Lorene called. "Now, Gina, your turn!"

Cool! Carli told herself. She jogged back to join the line. *Totally cool, in fact!*

She loved riding – she'd loped out to some great spots on horseback. Speed was Carli's thing, plus the balance and agility you needed to ride well. Then there was the sound of the horse's hooves thundering across green meadows, the fallen logs to jump, the crouching, swerving and bending to avoid low branches. All good.

But the thrill of hitting that springboard and throwing yourself at the table, of soaring into the air and perfecting your salto or your pike, of having only yourself, pure muscle and bone and determination, to rely on – that was something else.

Carli stood in line, breathing deeply, going through the next vault in her mind, rehearsing every movement.

"Good job, Gina. Great height there. Good vault. You're next, Tanya. Watch your run-up. Come on, girl, focus. Get ready and go!"

Nothing compares! Carli thought. *Give me the balance beam and the uneven bars, the vault and the floor exercise over riding any day!*

CHAPTER 2

"It's OK, I'm used to hard work," Carli told Lee.

It was Sunday morning. He'd found her lifting bales of hay onto the back of the Jeep and offered to help.

"Anyway, don't you have your own chores?" she asked with a grin.

Lee nodded. "Yeah — to help you put the hay in the feeders. Don's orders."

"Oh!" Carli's grin widened. "In that case, you lift while I stack."

Springing quickly from the tailboard onto the metal platform, she took the bales from Lee and hauled them up. When they'd finished, she clambered over the hay and swung into the cab, sitting beside

Lee as he started the engine.

"Hold on!" he yelled.

"Whoa!" she cried, hanging on tight as Lee drove the ancient truck from the barn out into the pastures. "What is this – the Indie 500?!"

Thirty horses came cantering for food. There were sorrels and paints, greys and Palaminos, all crowding round to get at their food. They munched greedily as Carli and Lee tossed hay into the metal feeders.

"So, Lee – where's home for you?" Carli asked as they drove the empty truck back to the barn.

"Chicago. But I came here for a year before college, to be with my dad."

Carli thought for a second, working it out. "OK, so your dad lives here in Colorado and your mom lives in Chicago?"

He nodded. "I'm a city boy. My dad and mom split when I was six years old. My dad drifted for a while, then landed here."

"Where exactly?" Carli thought Lee seemed cool – kind of shy, which she liked, and serious.

"In the Springs. I drive into town and see him on my days off."

"And how does a city boy like working on a ranch?"

Lee considered it. "I'm happy working with horses."

"But not with people?" she guessed.

He grinned and ducked his head. "I never said that. How about you, Carli? Do you like the cowboy life?"

She paused. "Same as you. The animals are cool. But anyway, I have to go clean cabins." Stepping down from the Jeep, she turned back to Lee. "Later on, I'm going to work with Diamond in the round pen. You could come and help if you have time."

"I'd like that," he said quietly. "But Don asked me to lead a kids' trail ride this afternoon. Sorry."

"No problem – see you around." Carli

headed for the laundry to pick up fresh sheets. She had six cabins to clean and fifteen beds to make before the new guests arrived at three o'clock. Then she had a date with Diamond. After that, she had to catch up on all the studying she'd missed on account of gymnastics camp. Carli sighed. Sometimes there weren't enough hours in the day.

Tanya called her at half past five. "Hey, Carli! Is there any chance you can make it into town tonight? Lorene says she can fit in an extra coaching session."

"No way!" Carli said, staring at the stack of schoolbooks on her table. "We've got twenty-three new guests in and I've been making beds all afternoon. I haven't even started my maths homework. It's crazy here."

"Poor you," her friend commiserated.

Carli looked out of her bedroom window, at Lee and her dad stacking more hay on the Jeep, at the horses grazing in the meadows and the mountains rising sheer out of the valley. In the distance, Sawtooth Lake glittered under a pink evening sun. "Yeah, it's a tough life," she said, half-joking, half-serious. "I'll tell you one thing for sure, Tanya – I'm coming to school tomorrow so I can have a break!"

Monday, and school was school – the same as always.

"...Carli Carroll, I want to see your maths homework. Please hand it in first thing tomorrow morning."

"...You need to improve your grade in history, Carli. With a little more effort, I'm sure you can do it."

"...Hey, Carli. Want to play tennis?"

School had ended and Carli and Tanya were getting ready to cycle across town to the gym. "Sorry, Matt, I have gymnastics tonight. Maybe tomorrow," she replied. Matt was really nice, but gymnastics had to come first as far as Carli was concerned.

They pedalled out through the school gates and cycled across the parking lot that adjoined the nearby mall. Taking a short cut, they arrived at the same time as their friend Gina and a new girl called Martha. They all went into the changing rooms together, chatting about the session ahead.

"Lorene wants us to work on the beam today," Tanya told them.

Gina groaned. "She wants me to work on my split jump, and I'm not up to that right now. I twisted my ankle."

"Tell her," Carli insisted. "Lorene's not a monster. She'll understand."

Some of the girls were scared of the coach, but not Carli. Sure, Lorene had a tough exterior and a voice like an army sergeant. And she hardly ever cracked a smile. But Carli knew it was a front – all Lorene ever wanted to do was to help you reach your true potential as a gymnast.

"I can't tell her. She'll say I'm wimping

out, especially since we've got the interstate competition in Denver coming up soon," Gina sighed. She flexed her sore ankle, then followed the others into the gym hall.

"Lorene sure seems fierce!" Martha muttered to Carli, hanging back. She'd spotted the coach handing out orders to a bunch of girls who'd arrived just before them.

"I want you out of your comfort zones, pushing your bodies just that little bit harder," the coach was insisting in her loud voice. "I know the balance beam is only four inches wide, but you have to attack it as if you're working on a floor exercise. You must be confident up there."

"She's not so fierce when you get to know her," Carli told Martha with a grin. "Come on, don't be scared."

Lorene turned to greet them. "Hey, girls, come join us! Gina, what's up?"

"Nothing. I'm OK."

Lorene studied Gina closely. "You're limping. What happened?"

"See, she spots the least little thing!" Carli told the new girl.

"I twisted my ankle playing basketball," Gina confessed.

Lorene nodded. "OK, so sit this out. Do some sit-ups, work on your upper-body strength, but don't put any strain on that ankle until you've seen the physio. In fact, Rick's in the treatment room, so go and do that right now!"

Relieved, Gina zipped up her top and limped away. Meanwhile, Lorene began her pep talk again.

"The balance beam – over sixteen feet of leather-covered sprung wood, four and a half feet above the floor, ninety seconds to impress the judges. It's a tough discipline and one you need to master if you're going to place at the interstate competition."

Let me get up there! Carli thought as Lorene coached.

"Tanya, when you work on your routine today, I want you to focus on covering the entire length of the beam. You lose points if you don't. Martha, why don't you get up there first and show us what you can do? Are you OK with that?"

Nodding anxiously, Martha went forward. Once on the beam, she drew up her slight body to full height, balanced on one skinny leg and went into a slow arabesque. Then she tilted backwards, arched her back and executed a back flip, followed by a lunge and a pivot, which threw her sideways into a serious wobble.

Lorene stepped quickly forward in case Martha fell. "OK?"

Martha nodded, breathed deep and took off from one foot into a graceful cat leap.

"She's got guts," Tanya said to Carli. "How old do you reckon she is? Younger than us — maybe eleven?"

Carli nodded. *Let me up there!* Eager to begin, she thought her way through her own beam routine — the cat leaps and the pivots, the body wave leading to a back handspring and then a back salto.

And today she wanted to include the extra 360-degree turn she'd been working on during her gymnastics trip. That would be a challenge – to fit it into the 90-second time limit and make it flow with the rest of her routine.

"OK, good!" Lorene told Martha, who dismounted from the beam and breathlessly awaited the verdict. "That's a pretty challenging routine, Martha – plenty for us to work on together."

The blonde kid's face lit up with relief. She nodded and trotted back to join the line.

"OK, Carli, I can see you champing at the bit over there," Lorene said. She gestured her forward. "Up you go!"

My turn! My chance to get it right! Let this be perfect!

Carli ran forward and vaulted onto the beam. She landed and the moment her bare feet touched the cool, polished surface, she felt at home. Like a high-wire walker, she stretched out her arms then drew them up over her head. *Attack the beam!* she thought. *Show no fear. Imagine you're performing your floor exercises.*

She arched forward into a slow, smooth handspring, then progressed from there into a quick salto, flipping head over heels. Then, with a twist of the upper body she made a 180-degree turn into a cabriole leap that wasn't quite high enough – then spun into a cartwheel.

Believe! Carli told herself. *Forget the fluffed cabriole, focus on the new 360-degree turn. Look ahead!*

She went on working, kept control, stretching every fibre in her body, flexing every muscle. *Bend, twist, balance. Leap, land and turn.* Everything here was to do with balance, keeping it together and not letting go. She nailed the 360, but had to rush through the central section of her routine, conscious of the seconds ticking away.

Then finally Carli was at the end of her routine and ending with a split jump into a forward flip with twist. She made a safe landing, head back, arms upstretched.

"Good work." Lorene's comment came with a "but" and Carli waited for her to go on. "Not sure about the extra turn. Let's think about it."

Tough love! Carli gritted her teeth and nodded. The coach had thirty years of experience. Lorene had seen it all and done it all herself – she'd even competed at Olympic level.

"OK, Tanya, you're up!"

"How did you do?" Gina asked Carli at the end of the session. She was still in the treatment room with the physio, having her ankle treated.

"Pretty good, except for my cabriole. That wasn't a hundred percent."

Gina grinned. "There's Little Miss Perfectionist for you!"

"Tell that to my maths teacher!" Carli laughed. She stayed there for a while, watching the physio gently tilt and flex Gina's injured ankle. He was a new guy at the gym – grey-haired but still in good shape, clean-shaven and wearing a black T-shirt and tracksuit bottoms.

"How's the ankle?" she asked Gina.

"Sore. Not too bad. Rick says I need to rest it for a week, which is such a bummer."

"Minimum," the physio emphasized with a stern look. "I'll see you again on Wednesday." He motioned for Gina to put her shoe back on.

"Hey, Rick, this is Carli Carroll." Gina made the introductions. "She's the best gymnast around here."

"Hi, Carli," Rick said, turning his back on her as he stuffed used towels into the laundry basket.

"Rick isn't exactly a talker," Gina explained as she and Carli left the room. "I got about fifty words out of him the whole time I was in there, and forty of them were grunts."

Carli smiled. "Hey, I came to offer you a ride home. Lee's picking me up. We could drive your way."

"Ooh, Lee!" Gina giggled. "Is he the guy who drove you into town last weekend?"

"He's my dad's new wrangler." Carli blushed, keen to play down Lee's good looks. "He gets all the short-straw jobs, like driving into town to pick me up."

"Yeah, *and* he's cute!" Gina insisted.

"And you're *walking* home if you don't stop fooling around." Carli searched the parking lot for the Triple X Jeep. She spotted the dusty brown wreck, then realized there was no driver. "Where's Lee got to?"

"Back there." Gina pointed over her shoulder towards the exit to the gym. "That's him, isn't it?"

Sure enough, Lee was leaning against the doorpost, hands in pockets, deep in conversation with Rick the non-communicative physio.

Both men seemed animated. Lee kept on asking questions, which the older man laughed off. Rick was spreading his palms flat and shrugging in a don't-ask-me way.

How come Lee's talking to Rick? Carli wondered.

"Do they know each other?" Gina asked.

"I don't know." Carli watched as Lee suddenly turned away and strode across the lot towards them.

"Hey, girls," he said, nodding shyly.

"Lee, can we give Gina a ride out to Redwood Park? It's on our route."

"Sure thing," he replied. He seemed reluctant to talk as Gina and Carli piled into the cab.

"So what's Lorene planning to get us to do on Wednesday?" Gina asked. "Bars or floor exercise?"

"Floor," Carli answered, sinking into her seat and strapping herself in.

"Pity. I might have been able to work on the bars, even with this ankle." Like Carli, Gina was super-keen. "Now it looks like I'll fall behind in my training programme. I might not make the interstate competition this summer after all."

"Yeah, you will," Carli insisted. "We both will!"

"You will, I so know you will!" Gina sighed, pushing her short, dark hair back from her forehead. "Like I was telling Rick earlier, you're the best under-16 gymnast in the whole of the Springs − probably even including Denver as well."

Mention of the physio's name seemed to bring a frown to Lee's face, but he drove on without comment.

Gina chatted on. "I told Rick he ought to take a look at you, Carli."

Carli shrugged. For the first time she noticed that Lee was uncomfortable with their conversation. She decided to charge in with her usual directness. "Hey Lee, I didn't realize you knew Rick until I saw you two having a conversation back there!"

Lee shrugged and turned onto the Redwood Park road.

"Stop here. This is my house!" Gina cried. She opened the door and jumped out of the cab.

"Remember that ankle!" Carli cried.

"Ouch!"

"Too late."

"See you tomorrow," Gina said with a wave, limping away.

Quickly Lee reversed into a driveway and turned the Jeep. Soon they were back on the highway.

"So how come you know him?" Carli persisted.

"Who?" Lee checked in his mirror.

"Rick," Carli said. "You know who!"

"Sure I know him," Lee conceded, speeding along the side of the clear river. Up ahead, the road rose steeply into the snow-capped mountains.

"How come?" Getting facts out of Lee was like winkling crayfish meat out of its shell. "Rick only just started work at the gym. So what's the link?"

Lee glanced sideways and narrowed his blue eyes, deciding to satisfy Carli's curiosity at last. "The link is — Rick Scottsdale is my father."

"Your father!" she echoed.

Lee nodded. "Yeah. Is that specific enough for you?"

CHAPTER 3

Lee and Rick Scottsdale – it was obviously a touchy subject and Carli avoided it when she got up early the next morning to school Diamond in the round pen.

"You want to watch me do the join-up?" she asked Lee when she spotted him saddling horses in the corral.

On the tackroom porch, Carli's dad and the head wrangler, Ben Adams, were chalking up names of guests beside the names of horses – Jennie Foster next to Gunsmoke, Art Foster next to Forrest Gump, and so on. They were getting ready to take the guests out for a ride and Lee was working flat out.

"I'll come over as soon as I've finished

here," Lee promised.

So Carli led the sorrel colt into the pen then let her off the halter rein. She sent her cantering around the edge of the pen, waiting for her to lower her head. "Good girl," she murmured. "You learn fast."

Diamond's head went down sooner than before. Then she turned in towards Carli, waiting for her next move.

Carli stood patiently, avoiding eye contact, expecting the colt to approach in her own time.

Diamond looked long and hard at the still figure in the centre of the pen. She flicked her ears and sniffed the air then gingerly took a step towards Carli.

Out of the corner of her eye Carli noticed her dad and Ben come up to the fence to watch, but she didn't take her attention off the colt, not even for a second. *Come on, Diamond, I'm not gonna hurt you!* she thought. *You can trust me, I promise!*

Perhaps the young horse remembered the early days when Carli had hand-reared her and cared for her after her mom had died. In any case, she came smoothly forward, neck stretched out, nostrils quivering.

"Good girl!" Carli breathed.

Diamond was only a step away, growing bolder by the second. When Carli slowly raised her arm, she shied a fraction but then held steady while Carli reached out to stroke her face.

"Easy, girl. You're so good. I'm just gonna fasten this halter on – you know what it is, you've worn it before. Yeah, good girl!"

With the rope halter on and the colt nuzzling up to her, Carli knew that her morning's job was done. Diamond had joined up.

"Nice work!" Lee called from the fence. He'd joined the other two men to watch Carli work with Diamond.

"Don't you believe it," Don Carroll muttered as he moved off with Ben.

"Carli's new-fangled technique takes way too long. I go for the good old sacking-out method – tie a sack on their backs and run 'em into the ground till they can't move no more. Then slap a saddle on 'em."

"Yeah, thanks, Dad!" Carli stood up to him. "That's so not the modern way!"

"I was impressed," Lee chipped in. "I reckon Carli – "

Don cut him short. "Yeah, well go and be impressed back in the tackroom. There's bridles to clean and fit before the guests come down."

Working with Diamond, standing up to her dad, driving into town, drifting through the school day then back home to more ranch work – this was Carli's routine for Monday and Tuesday.

"You're getting more than your fair share of driving me into town," she said to Lee on the Wednesday morning. "You must be bored out of your skull with this route."

"It's OK," Lee told her. "Anyway, today's my day off. I get to stay in town and hang out."

"With your dad?" she asked. She opened her mouth and the question fell out without her brain kicking in. *Touchy subject, remember.*

"Maybe," Lee grunted. "I got errands to run. I might take in a movie."

"But you'll be there to drive me home after my gymnastics class?" Carli checked. "I should be finished at 6.30, if that's OK."

Lee pulled up at the school gates. "See you then," he said. "Have a good day."

"I *won't!*" she assured him. "At least, not until I get out on that gym floor!"

The floor exercise was the high point of gymnastics for Carli – the pinnacle, the peak, the spot where everything came together. On the floor she could dance – really dance. She could be the acrobat. She could be herself!

Her music began. The violins jumped and jigged as Carli sprang into action with a series of handsprings combined with Cossack leaps and pivots across the diagonal. They were high-speed, medium-difficulty moves, still building momentum.

Rick Scottsdale joined Lorene in the gym, watching Carli's performance.

"Good energy," he said. "Good sense of rhythm."

Carli stopped at the very edge of the floor, stretched both arms high, and as the music continued to race, she went into a body wave and then a series of quick steps into a half-in, half-out salto, giving a half twist on each flip – down into a plié as the music calmed and a deep cello took over from the violins – a relevé, slow and graceful, another pivot and a slow walkover, walking through the air as her hands took her weight.

"Carli is very supple," Lorene said. "And strong. Good control. For sure, she's got what it takes."

Carli's momentum was still building; she was travelling low across the floor, waiting for those soaring violins to return. *Now for the three connected saltos – up, head over heels and twist, again and again! Turn and tumble this way. Turn again and tumble.* She ran at the triple twist – the climax – gathering speed, aiming to rotate her whole body three times in the air, flinging herself into it, spinning and landing in perfect balance.

"Brave," Rick said to Lorene. "The girl has guts."

Winding down, turning and tilting, putting in leaps and pirouettes, ending with a split leap and down onto both knees, arms outstretched.

Breathless, smiling – free!

Rick nodded and disappeared into the treatment room.

After the class, Lorene collared Carli. "Did

you pinpoint any faults in your routine tonight?" she asked.

"No – leastways, not in execution. My rhythm was OK, too." Carli zipped up her jacket and thrust her legs into her workout trousers. "How about my presentation? Did *you* see anything?"

"Me, personally? No, I didn't," Lorene said slowly, as if a new idea had occurred to her. "But how would you like an expert opinion?"

Carli smiled. "That would be you, Lorene, wouldn't it?"

"OK then – *another* expert opinion. If you don't mind, I'd like you to come with me."

"Lead the way."

Still puzzled, Carli followed the coach out of the gym, past the door to the shower room, along a corridor stacked with apparatus and weights, until they came to the treatment room.

Lorene knocked on the door. "Rick, can we come in?"

There was a short pause before the physiotherapist opened the door. He didn't let them into the room, but stood barring their way. "What is it, Lorene? I'm busy writing up case notes."

"This won't take long, Rick. I know you had some comments on Carli's performance when we were watching her floor exercise earlier. Do you have any advice to give her?"

Carli couldn't help frowning. What could Rick Scottsdale possibly know about women's gymnastics that Lorene hadn't covered?

The physio's face showed no reaction. His thin lips stayed set in a straight line and his blue eyes were fixed on the floor. "You don't need my advice, Lorene," he muttered. "You know what you're doing better than anyone I can think of. Always did."

"But a fresh eye is good," the coach insisted. "Carli would really appreciate it if you gave your opinion."

I would? Carli thought. This was only her third sight of Rick Scottsdale. So far, she wasn't particularly impressed.

Rick shrugged and glanced briefly at Carli. He seemed to catch the hostility in her eyes and looked back at her with a little more interest.

"Rick was in the US team with me at the Montreal Olympics, way back in '76," Lorene explained to Carli. "He was a total genius in the rings event. That's why I invited him here to work as a physio."

Carli's jaw dropped. No way had she expected this. The Olympic Games in 1976 were the golden games — when Nadia Comaneci, Carli's all-time heroine, had scored her perfect 10s. And Lorene was telling her that Rick had been a part of all that!

"So come on, Rick, tell us what you saw in Carli's performance," Lorene invited.

"Challenging routine." He shrugged, still

reluctant to cooperate. "Who did the choreography?"

"I did," Lorene answered. "But Carli worked out her own strengths – especially the flowing energy she builds up in the middle section. She has natural grace, don't you think?"

Rick nodded. "I'd pick out the slow walkover – it was as good as it gets. Variety in the routine was good. The triple twist was way up there at international level."

Carli stared at the grey-haired ex-gymnast. Though his voice was flat and his expression gave nothing away, he had obviously been paying attention, as he was picking out the highlights of her routine.

"We'd like to know how you rated the overall presentation and artistry." Lorene wouldn't let Rick off the hook just yet. She wanted to squeeze every scrap of advice out of him.

And now Rick did look Carli straight in

the eye. "Still some work needed there," he said bluntly.

"Hmm." At last Lorene had pinned him down.

"What kind of work?" Carli asked quickly. If there was anything that needed improvement, she wanted to know.

"You have to let your personality come through," Rick told her. "Right now, you're way too serious. You need more bounce."

"Bounce . . . right!" Lorene said, as if she suddenly saw what he was saying.

Unexpectedly, Rick's criticism stung Carli. She frowned and looked down before mumbling a farewell to her coach and heading for the door.

"Right on target, as usual, Rick," Lorene confirmed, watching Carli turn and walk back down the corridor, her head hanging. "I'll say this for you – you may be down on your luck right now, old friend, but you've still got the best eye in the business!"

★ ★ ★

"You never said your dad was a gymnast," Carli said to Lee on the ride home. She was still feeling sore over the negative comment about her presentation.

"You never asked," Lee replied. "Anyhow, it was a long time ago. Way before I was born."

"Lorene says he was good."

Lee shrugged. He stopped at the gas station to refuel. When he came back, he handed Carli a pack of gum. "So how's Diamond coming along?" he asked.

"She's doing good." Carli clocked the change of subject and took the hint. "I'll use the round pen to put a saddle on her tomorrow morning early."

Lee nodded. "I hope to be there. I like the way you work with the colts, Carli. I reckon being a horse trainer would be a pretty neat job for you when you leave school."

"Yeah, but it isn't what I want. Gymnastics is my thing. It's all I ever wanted to do, since I was eight years old."

They drove on in silence, turning off onto the dirt road, catching glimpses of Silverfish Creek between the trees.

"But how long does it last?" Lee asked after a long silence.

"How long does what last?"

"Being a top gymnast. A couple of years – three or four if you're lucky. Then what?"

To Carli the answer was obvious. "Then you learn to be a judge or a coach. You stay involved. Listen, Lee – you think training colts would be neat. Well, I happen to believe that training young gymnasts would be better. Like Lorene. She has a cool life."

"Yeah? What if you can't stay involved? Not everyone can be a coach. What if you have to drop out?"

Why the third degree? Carli wondered. How come shy Lee was ramming the questions down her throat? "Like your dad, you mean?"

Lee nodded. "He was top man on the rings, yet I look at him now and I worry about him. He doesn't have any direction in his life."

"I get you," Carli said. Lee didn't reply and Carli sat back, looking out of the window, respecting Lee's silence as the Jeep jolted over the rutted surface and past the Five Mile Post.

CHAPTER 4

"You were flying today, Carli." Gina picked up her towel after practising her routine on the uneven bars. "Those release moves were really something."

"Thanks." Carli felt happy with her Saturday morning's work. "How's your ankle?"

"Much better. I have to see Rick now for another treatment, but I could meet up with you and Tanya later if you want to grab a drink."

"Talking of Rick . . . " Tanya came up behind them and pointed out the physio standing in the doorway, apparently waiting for Gina. "How come he keeps watching you, Carli?"

Carli was startled. "What do you mean?"

"He was there earlier, while you were on the bars. It was as if he was a judge, scoring your every move. As soon as your routine was over, he moved off."

Carli felt herself stiffen. No doubt the physio had spotted more flaws in her performance. "Believe it or not, he used to compete as an Olympic gymnast," she told them. "In '76, alongside Lorene."

"Wow! You wouldn't think it to look at the guy now." Tanya shook her head. "He seems kind of – boring!"

"Pretty grey – Mr Average," Gina agreed.

From their huddle by the bars, Tanya looked Rick over. "Mr *Below* Average. I mean, what *is* he wearing? That tracksuit top definitely came out of a charity shop!"

"Shh!" Even though she wasn't a fan of Rick Scottsdale, Carli was uncomfortable with this girly giggling. When Gina went off with Rick and Lorene called Carli across, she was glad to escape.

"So, Carli!" the coach began. "Another excellent morning's work. Neat dismounts, exciting transitions."

Carli nodded and waited for the next piece of analysis from her long-time trainer. Instead, there was silence.

"I've been thinking," Lorene began again after the longest pause. "And I've decided that I've taught you just about all I can in this group situation."

Carli blinked, then tilted her head to one side. "What are you saying?"

"I'm saying you need to move on," Lorene replied, guiding Carli towards the exit. "If you're going to make it to the next level, especially after the competition in Denver, you need one-to-one tuition. You need someone to work out a diet and strength-building programme exclusively for you – someone who will work to improve the fine details of your routines. I can't do that when I need to work with newcomers like Martha."

Carli frowned, trying to work out what Lorene was leading up to. Was there an ulterior motive behind her words? What was the hidden agenda? She didn't have to wait long to find out.

"How does this sound to you?" Lorene asked. "How about Rick stepping up and helping me with your coaching from now on? He could do all the stuff I've been talking about."

"Rick?" Carli echoed.

"You don't need to decide right away," Lorene said hurriedly. "I'm just floating the idea. Rick hasn't always been a physio. He got his professional coaching certificates way back, so that's not a problem. And trust me, he's an amazing guy. He'd bring out the best in you, without a doubt."

Carli's head was in a spin. "This is pretty sudden," she stammered. "I mean, you and I – we've worked together since I was eight. You know me better than anyone."

Lorene nodded. "Sure, and I won't stop

working with you. I'll be alongside Rick every step of the way. But maybe you and I have gotten too cosy. I reckon you need to be pushed a little – you know, taken out of your comfort zone. Rick would definitely do that."

"Let me think about it." Carli needed to buy herself some time.

"Sure, no rush. I haven't even spoken to Rick about it yet. And it's a big decision for both of you." There was another long pause. Then Lorene said, "I reckon you can make it all the way to the top, Carli."

"You do?" Carli's heart flipped and twisted like it was doing a floor exercise all on its own.

"To the very top – to the Olympics and beyond."

"Wow!" A pathetic, little-kid word to convey the excitement she was feeling, Carli knew.

"If . . . " Lorene said slowly. "*If* you get the coaching now. If you're pushed and honed, put into the right competitions within the state of Colorado and across the country, so that the selectors notice you. You hear what I'm saying?"

Flip-flop went Carli's heart. Her pulse raced.

"So think about it," Lorene said finally.

"I will," Carli promised.

"And let me know on Monday."

The Olympics and beyond! Carli repeated Lorene's words to herself as she worked with Diamond in the round pen. Even now it made her heart race. It was what she'd dreamed of but never dared to put into words — her heart's desire.

"You're so smart, Diamond," she murmured, as the colt did a willing join-up. She ran her hands down the smooth neck and through the pale-honey mane. "Now look, I'm going to show you this saddle blanket — I'm just slipping it across your back, no problem!"

Diamond's whole body quivered as she felt the blanket rest across her back. For a few seconds she couldn't understand the weird new sensation.

"Carli, can you come and help in the kitchen when you're through out there?" Beth Carroll called from the house porch. "We've got a whole heap of breakfast orders stacking up."

The Olympics! But it would mean working with Rick Scottsdale, who she didn't know and who, let's face it, she didn't even like.

"Carli, you heard what your mom said." Don Carroll interrupted her work with Diamond. "You hand that colt over to me *now* and go help in the kitchen!"

Carli nodded and washed her hands before getting stuck into breakfasts — making pancakes, cooking bacon until it crisped, serving eggs over easy to a dozen hungry, talkative guests. Then she headed out again to the round pen, to find that her dad had handed over to Lee.

"Hey, Lee," she said. "You got Diamond's saddle on. That's cool!"

He smiled and nodded. "What next, Miss Horse Trainer?"

"Watch," she told him, stepping up into the nearest stirrup and relaxing her body across Diamond's saddle. "See, she's learning to take my weight, but she's not ready to let me swing a leg over and sit."

Uneasy at yet another fresh sensation, little Diamond skittered sideways and Carli quickly slipped to the ground. "I guess that's enough pressure for today. Do you want to help me brush her down, then feed her?"

Lee glanced at his watch. "I haven't eaten breakfast yet."

"Oh, OK, I can manage here."

"No, it's cool. I'll skip the food and maybe get it later."

Together Lee and Carli led Diamond into the corral and began work with the brushes.

"Hey, Carli, your dad wants you to lead a trail ride this morning!" Ben Adams called from the bunkhouse.

"Cool, no problem," she yelled back.

She and Lee soon finished grooming Diamond and led her into the feed stall. "Just time to pick up a snack!" Carli told him.

So they headed for the kitchen for a stack of pancakes. "Thanks for your help, Lee," she said, her mouth full.

"No problem."

She looked at him across the bare table and made a quick decision. After all, who else could she confide in? "Hey Lee, I hope you don't mind me talking about your dad."

"Again?" he said with a wry smile.

"Again," she nodded. "Sorry. But I have this — what would you call it? This dilemma! And you might be able to help me out."

Lee stopped eating and looked serious.

"Go on," he said.

"Your dad – Rick – he used to be a coach, didn't he?"

Lee nodded. "Way back, yeah."

"Well, now my trainer, Lorene, thinks your dad should step in and start coaching me one-to-one."

"She does?" Lee lost interest in his breakfast and stood up to stare out of the window.

"She says he would help me get to the very top in gymnastics – and I really, really want that to happen."

"Yeah."

"So I wondered what you thought about the idea. Like, should I take a risk and get the extra coaching? Or should I stick with Lorene?"

"You're asking me to tell you about my dad?" Lee said slowly. He came back to the table and sat down. "Even though you might not like what you hear?"

"Go for it!" she said firmly, wondering

what the young rancher was going to say.

"OK. I never saw it for myself, but from what I hear, my dad was a top-class gymnast. But he was a lousy father."

Carli nodded. "I guessed as much."

"He was never there for me," Lee went on. "He was always off on some trip to Wisconsin or Iowa, looking for the next international gold-medal winner. And when he was home, he wasn't interested in Mom or me – not really. He was trying to sell food supplements and working on training programmes all the time, aiming to produce the superman or superwoman who would beat the Russians and the Romanians."

"Did he ever succeed?" Carli asked.

Lee shook his head. "And he never earned any money out of it, either. The sport ate him up and spat him out again, without any direction or anything left to live for. But the problem was, he couldn't let go."

"Of what?"

"Of being there, way back in Montreal, of representing his country and being at the top of his game."

"So he couldn't get past competing in the Olympics?" Carli said, beginning to understand.

Lee frowned and fell silent. "My mom always said that life was a balancing act — like being on the beam and trying not to fall off. One wrong move and you were done. Well, Dad's wrong move was to get hooked on his Olympic memories. For years and years. And every year he earned less — even when I was a little kid, Mom had to work hard to pay the bills."

"So your mom was trying her best to keep it together."

"Yeah. She didn't blame him. But in the end, they broke up. I stayed with Mom. Dad lost everything."

"Because he didn't balance gymnastics with the rest of his life," Carli concluded.

Lee had answered some of her questions, but now she had a whole lot more — and number one was, did she want to be coached by a guy who had wrecked his family and his whole life because of his gymnastic dreams?

"Yeah," Lee agreed. "Mom still worries about him. That's why she wanted me to spend some time with him down here — so I could keep an eye on him."

"That's real big of her," Carli murmured. "So how's it working out?"

Lee managed a small grin. "Let's just say I'm still worried."

"And it's big of *you* to tell me about it," Carli added. "I hope you didn't mind me asking. I appreciate it."

"It's OK. I got a load of stuff off my chest," he said, starting to clear away the plates. "Hey, Carli, about this coaching stuff — it's still your choice, you know. You do what's best for you."

"Thanks anyway." Seeing Ben through

the window, and hearing her mom talking to her dad out in the reception hall, she knew it was time to move.

"We're down to fifteen guests next week and thirteen the week after," Beth was saying as she consulted the booking sheets. "I know it's early in the season, but that's still not enough."

"Too many bills, too few guests," Don muttered. "The old, old story."

Carli sighed as she stood up and followed Lee to the corral. She felt unsettled by his story, surrounded by problems that she couldn't solve.

So where does that leave me? she asked herself. *Do I chase my dream, or do I stick with my folks and help out all I can, because it doesn't look to me like I can do both, the way Mom and Dad have me working all hours. Do I reach for the stars or keep my feet on the ground?*

"OK, here we go – another day, another dollar," Don said, striding after Carli and fixing his dusty Stetson firmly on his head.

Feet on the ground, counting the cash, making ends meet. She sighed, then gazed up at the big blue sky. "OK, forget it," she said. "Even if everything else was simple, there's no way my parents could afford to pay for extra coaching from Rick Scottsdale. No way in this world!"

CHAPTER 5

That evening, Carli called Lorene.

"Hey, Carli!" Lorene sounded surprised. She turned down the background noise from the TV. "What's up?"

"Lorene, I've been thinking through what we talked about yesterday. The Rick Scottsdale idea."

"Good. Did you talk it through with your folks yet?"

"No. But listen, that's the thing. My mom and dad – you know, we don't have a lot of money. The ranch isn't doing too well right now."

"I hear you, Carli. But don't worry about that angle. I already discussed it with Rick. He says it's not a problem."

Carli felt a dart of anger run through her. "Hey, listen, I thought we were waiting until Monday before we took it any further!"

"We were," Lorene agreed. "But Rick must be a mind-reader. How else do you figure out the fact that he came to me this afternoon and floated the idea of taking you on as his student in the build-up to the interstate competition next month?"

"He did?" Lorene's news had completely taken the wind out of Carli's sails. She'd picked up the phone with what she was going to say all planned out – *Hey, Lorene. I've been thinking through the Rick Scottsdale idea. I don't reckon it would work. I'm sorry but I'm going to have to say no . . .*

"Yeah. As a matter of fact, Rick is here now, sitting in front of my TV as we speak. He came over an hour ago and asked me if I thought it would be a good idea if he started coaching you, one-to-one."

"That's weird!" Carli stammered.

"Big coincidence," Lorene agreed. "I told him right away that your folks weren't exactly loaded — I hope you don't mind, Carli. Rick said it wasn't about the money. He'd spotted a quality in you that could take you far."

"He had?" Carli didn't usually sound like such a dope. But this thing was speeding out of her control. All her reasons to say no were dissolving like sugar lumps in hot tea.

"So," Lorene went on, "as far as payment for the coaching goes, Rick is happy not to take any extra. All you have to do is pay me for the group lessons and Rick and I will split it fifty-fifty. He won't take a cent more, and if you don't believe me, I'll put him on so you can talk to him." Her voice faded as she handed over the phone.

"No, don't do that!" Carli protested loudly. Too late. Rick cleared his throat.

"Hey, Carli. Looks like Lorene and I had the same idea," he said with a short laugh.

"No, really — I'd be more than happy to teach you. Actually, it'd be a privilege."

This was too much! Carli held the phone away from her ear and tried to think. *It's not just the cash we're short on, it's time as well, remember!* She held the phone close again. "I don't know, Rick. I'm really busy. I have to put in a lot of work for my mom and dad here on the ranch."

Plus, there's the back-story I got from Lee earlier. I don't want my life to fall out of balance like yours did. That would be seriously scary! But she couldn't say this straight out. It would have to lie below the surface.

"It sure is a big commitment," Rick agreed. "But you know the old saying — if you want something done, ask a busy person. I'm a believer in that."

"Well, I guess maybe I could fit in a few extra lessons during the week," Carli said slowly.

"We could take it easy at first — see if we

get along," Rick suggested. "Not all coaching relationships are made in heaven. We'd have to wait and see."

Fair enough. "And you reckon you could help me take some big steps forward?" she asked, feeling suddenly shy.

There was a pause. Dialogue from the TV filtered through. "I could teach you what I know, and that's just about every aspect of this sport you can think of," Rick assured her, quietly confident without coming across as a loudmouth. "And I could show you the world of top-level gymnastics. We could hit plenty of competitions, build up your confidence. Who knows where it would lead?"

To the Olympics! Carli closed her eyes, trying not to be blinded by the bright lights that beckoned. *To competing with the world's top gymnasts . . . to achieving the perfect 10!*

"Carli, are you still there?" Rick asked.

"I'm here."

"Think about it some more. Maybe tomorrow you could come to the gym after school as usual and while Lorene works with the group, we could head off and look at your floor exercise. We'll pull it apart and put it back together with a little more fun and personality on view, like I said."

Carli nodded. "OK," she said.

"Good, see you then."

"Yeah, see you tomorrow."

"OK, goodbye for now, Carli."

"Goodbye."

How did that happen? Carli thought in the silence after she put down the phone. *Did I just get myself a new coach in spite of everything?*

Oh wow, yes, I guess I did!

"Now Carli, you're young and you still have some growing to do." Rick said before they began.

On the other side of the gym, Lorene worked with Tanya, Gina, Martha and the others.

"Anyhow, I reckon you'll stay below five foot five. You'll probably build up a little additional muscle, but not too much. You're a natural ectomorph."

"I am?" Carli was nervous. She seemed to be walking through a door she'd never been through before.

Rick smiled. "That means you're a skinny kid who doesn't easily put on weight. It's to do with genetics."

"That makes sense – my mom's small and thin."

"And you have excellent flexibility, plus stamina."

"You can tell all this just from watching me a couple of times?" Carli was impressed. She began to feel less scared.

"All this, plus a lot more. But what I haven't had a chance to work out yet is what's inside that head of yours. What makes you tick, Carli?"

She stared back at him as if he was speaking a foreign language. No one had ever asked her this before. "I have no idea!" she said.

"OK, so what makes you happy – besides gymnastics?"

She thought hard. "Riding bareback through Silverfish Creek. Being out alone, halfway up a mountain."

"Sounds neat," Rick agreed. "Freedom, huh?"

She nodded.

"So now we can begin. Carli loves freedom. Freedom is what we have to express in the dance moves of this floor exercise. I want to see you reach for the sky."

She nodded and got into position for the start of her routine.

"We know you can go through the moves pretty much without fault," Rick reminded her. "That's the easy part. Now try to capture that feeling you have out there on the mountain – with no one around. Just endless space, pure white snow, blue sky . . . "

Rick put on Carli's music, then stood back.

She took a deep breath and waited for the violins. They sounded like water running through the creek, like birds soaring overhead. She kept the pictures in her head and began.

The handsprings flowed, the Cossack leaps across the diagonal seemed to make her fly. Then the body wave – like birds' wings spreading and lifting her high, giving her momentum for the salto and through into the slow section, as if the white-water creek had hit a smooth, slowly winding section – a little bit sad as well as calm, with the cello's deep notes pulling at her heart strings. Her whole body swayed and bent to the rhythm; the walkover was smooth as silk.

Rick took in every detail – the angle of Carli's head, the extension of her fingertips, the expression on her face. "Now have fun!" he called, as the music quickened again.

A bubbling stream, light sparkling on the water, running on forever. Carli saw the picture as she went into the connected saltos. She felt the speed and the lightness as she tumbled this way and that. And now her triple twist, which should feel difficult, but this time came as naturally as breathing – a rapid sprint across the floor, leaping and twisting three times, landing with a sense of total, soaring joy!

"Well?" Lorene asked as she met up with Carli and Rick after the session.

Rick didn't answer but turned towards Carli with a questioning look.

She was still breathless, still flying. She nodded and smiled.

"Good, huh?" Lorene checked with Rick.

"'Good' doesn't cover what I just saw," he told her. His normally expressionless blue eyes were lit up with excitement. "'Magic' might do it. Or try 'One in a million'!"

Carli's eyes sparkled. She could hardly believe her ears.

Lorene gave a satisfied nod. Then she put an arm around Carli's shoulders. "So at last you think you found your golden girl, Rick?"

"Maybe," he said, as the elation faded and caution crept in. Then his certainty over Carli's talent broke back through. "You bet!" he said. "We're going to take this girl to Denver. She's going to be a star!"

Carli sang in the shower. Tingly clean, having changed into jeans and a T-shirt, she floated out of the changing room, down the corridor and out into the parking lot, where she found Lee.

"How was training?" he asked.

"Cool. Your dad's an amazing coach."

Lee smiled ruefully. "Maybe I should've been a gymnast," he said quietly. "That way I'd sure have seen a lot more of him!"

"Did something just happen between you and your dad?" Carli asked.

"Yeah, he didn't show up to Pizza Hut at 4.30. Turns out he was too busy coaching you. He forgot. Anyway, are you ready to go home?"

"Yes, but I was expecting to get a ride with Ben." She felt lousy about being the reason for Rick's no-show.

"I already called Ben to say I'd got it," Lee explained, striding off towards the Jeep.

Rick shouted after Carli. "See you Wednesday, 4 p.m. Balance-beam practice. Don't be late."

CHAPTER 6

"What's eating you?" Don Carroll asked Carli when she and Lee arrived home.

"Nothing," she replied, striding along the porch into the ranch house.

It had been a long, silent drive, with Lee cocooned in a shell of silence and Carli still experiencing twinges of guilt.

"Did you say thanks to Lee for the ride?" her father called after her.

"Thanks, Lee!" Carli let the door slam shut.

Inside the house, her mom was at the computer, working at a balance sheet showing complex figures and columns of profit and loss. "Hey, Carli," she said absently. Then, "Shoot!" as she clicked the wrong button and her figures disappeared. "I need a break," she sighed.

"I'll get you some coffee," Carli offered, disappearing into the kitchen.

Beth soon followed. "How was school?" she asked wearily.

"Same old," Carli mumbled. As usual, she'd been late handing in work, and as usual she was in trouble. "But hey, I have good news."

"You do?" Beth accepted the coffee gratefully then slumped in a chair. "I'm glad you have, Carli, 'cos I sure don't. I've been staring at those figures for a full hour, and no way can I get them to look OK for the bank."

"So, my *good* news," Carli persisted, sitting across the table from her mom. "I got myself a new gymnastics coach."

"You did?"

Hey, that's terrific news, honey! I'm real glad for you, the rosy-cheeked voice said.

"Well, I guess Lorene actually found him

for me," Carli explained. "It's a guy called Rick. She knows him from way back."

"So why bother changing coaches?" Beth asked, pinching the bridge of her nose to ease a headache.

In her parallel universe, Carli pictured her mom bright-eyed and glowing with pleasure, eager to hear every detail. *Go ahead, tell me all about it. This is so exciting!*

"I'm not switching coaches exactly. Lorene will still be there and we'll work as a team. But Rick can give me one-to-one attention. He's going to work out a unique training programme with me. I don't have to wait in line."

Beth sighed, then sipped at her coffee. "Jeez, Carli, stop right there. Before you say any more, what's this Rick guy going to charge us for the privilege of one-on-one teaching?"

"Zero. The cost is the same as it is for working with Lorene." Carli had expected this and came right in with the answer. "How cool is that?"

Her mom shook her head slightly. "The same? How does that work?"

"Rick is asking for what Lorene gets — not a penny more."

"But I mean, how does it work for him? Why would he do that?"

Carli had held on to her temper so far, but now she flared up. "Mom, you're so suspicious! I mean, does everyone have to have a bad reason for doing something good? Can't it just be that he likes my work and wants to help me improve?"

"Yeah, but you're still a kid and you're naive," Beth reminded her, quickly tiring of the argument. She got up to leave. "And I'm your mother, so I have to look out for you."

Carli followed her out onto the porch. "You're not saying I can't do this!" she begged. "Please, Mom, don't do that!"

"Not now, Carli, I don't have time." Beth

tried to push past Carli, who stood in her way.

"OK, OK!" Carli had to think fast. "Listen, Rick isn't just any guy. He was a top gymnast. If you don't believe me, we could Google him. He'd be up there on screen for you to take a look at. Come back inside and take a look!"

Her mom hesitated. "Maybe later," she conceded.

But Carli wouldn't let it drop. She followed Beth from the porch, out across the yard towards the corral. "And here's another reason. Rick's second name is Scottsdale. Rick Scottsdale – Lee Scottsdale – get it? Rick is Lee's dad. You like Lee, don't you? So you'll like Rick too."

Carli bit her lip. On second thoughts maybe this last part was a mistake. Now she had to keep her fingers crossed that her mom wouldn't march straight up to Lee and ask him his opinion of his dad.

So she gabbled on, trying to fill the

silence. "And he's a really cool guy. He was an Olympic athlete way back in '76, so he knows what he's talking about. Plus, he's doing it for practically nothing. What's not to like?"

Slowly her mom's mood softened. "I hear you," she muttered.

"So?" Carli ran in front to stop her opening the corral gate.

"So maybe I'll call Lorene to talk it through with her," Beth conceded.

"When?" Carli pestered. "Tonight, Mom. Do it tonight!"

"Later, when I have time. Now go and start your homework, and give me some peace!"

"What's the worst thing that could happen while you're up there balancing on that beam?" Rick asked Carli on Wednesday after school.

So far Beth Carroll hadn't got around to calling Lorene to discuss the new coaching situation. On the other hand, she hadn't said no to Rick either. So, impetuous as ever, Carli had taken this as a yes and gone right ahead.

"The worst thing?" she echoed, pressing the balls of her feet into the narrow beam and standing on tiptoe. "That's easy – I could fall off!"

"And then what?" her new coach insisted.

"I get a 0.5 deduction."

"What else?"

"I could break a leg, which isn't as bad as breaking my back if I fell off the bars during a high-flying release, I guess. But I still prefer the bars."

"What is it about the bars that you like? Tell me right away – off the top of your head."

"Speed," she answered. "Once I'm up there, I never stop moving."

"But on the beam you have to slow it down, strike a pose, to show the judges that you're in control?"

Carli nodded. "Too much time to think."

"Which means your natural way of doing stuff is to rush at it and use your instinct?"

"I guess." It was the first time Carli had ever had to analyse these things, but now Rick mentioned it, he was right on target, as usual. "Thinking isn't my strong point. Ask my teachers!"

Rick grinned. "OK, so on the beam we need to keep you moving – flowing from one move into the next. Let's start with the 360-degree turn element that you just introduced. Do you want to do it on one foot or one knee?"

"The left knee," Carli decided quickly.

"Good. Then you can change level through a push-up arch into standing and then down again into the splits. Let's see how that works."

No problem. Carli had listened carefully to the instruction and performed it without fault.

Rick stood back and clapped his hands. "Carli, you were born on a balance beam, I swear!"

"Thanks," Carli mumbled, a little embarrassed at the coach's praise. "What do you want to do next? Do you want to see my 180-degree leap or my forward handspring into salto?"

"Your diet is high on protein and carbs but low on vitamins and way too high in processed sugar," Rick pointed out on the following Saturday. He'd asked Carli to write down everything she'd eaten between Wednesday and Saturday and now he was inspecting her sheet while the group worked with Lorene. "Where's the fruit?" he asked. "Where are the vegetables?"

"There." Carli pointed to Thursday evening. "See? French fries. Potatoes are vegetables!"

"Yeah, right! Listen, I'm going to put you on vitamin supplements." Rick pulled down a couple of brown plastic jars from the shelf in the treatment room. "You have to take these three times a day, with every meal. OK, now tell me what exercise you get when you're not working here in the gym."

"How long have you got?" Carli asked. She'd already put in ninety minutes of work with Rick and Lorene on the uneven bars. The time had flown and yet again her new coach had been full of praise. But now she needed to shower and hurry to meet her mom outside the vet's clinic.

"Plenty, huh?" Rick asked.

"OK, let's see. I'm on horseback for three hours a day, minimum – five or six over the weekends and during vacations. I train the new colts. I scoop poop in the corral. I haul hay bales onto the back of the Jeep . . ."

"OK, enough. I forgot you live on a

ranch. How's that moody son of mine shaping up?"

The good-natured question took Carli by surprise. "Lee? He's cool."

"Tell him to answer my phone calls, would you? Say he's even worse than I am for keeping in touch, and I'm the first to admit I'm not the greatest."

"Sure," Carli promised half-heartedly. "But I haven't seen much of him lately either. Listen, sorry Rick, but I have to go."

"OK, so tomorrow would you like to put in an extra session on the vault?" he asked quickly. "Then we'll have run through all four events and we'll do a major evaluation to see where we go next."

"If I can get a ride into town on a Sunday," she agreed. "I'll call you and let you know."

Rick looked hard at her. "Or you can chill tomorrow if that's what you'd rather do. Don't let me push you too hard."

Carli looked up to meet his gaze. Her

clear brown eyes stared straight into his narrowed blue ones. "No, I want to work on my vault. I'll get a ride with Ben when he comes in to church," she promised.

"Good girl. We'll put in some extra difficulty, to increase your start values for Denver and the interstate."

"Sounds cool," she nodded.

"So get a good night's sleep," Rick called after her as she sped off towards the showers.

It had been a good morning. Carli had been relaxed while she'd shown Rick her routine on the uneven bars, swinging with perfect rhythm and transferring with split-second timing from low bar to high bar then back again.

As she'd told Rick on Wednesday, she loved the speed and thrill of swinging from the high bar, using the momentum to twist up into a handstand, transferring her weight, swinging down again, straight and true, gathering speed until she flipped off the bar with a perfect dismount.

But now, as she crossed Main Street and headed for the meeting with her mom outside the vet's, she knew from one look at Beth's face that the merry mood was about to change.

"So what kept you?" Beth demanded, tapping her wristwatch. "We said noon. It's ten after."

"Sorry. Rick was running through my diet sheet with me."

"Rick?" Her mom searched her memory. "Oh yeah, Mr Nice Guy. The one who's teaching you for peanuts. Listen, I didn't speak to Lorene yet."

Carli hurried down Main Street after her mom. At times like this it was best to say nothing.

"It's way down today's list, let me tell you, after picking up these vaccination certificates from the vet, calling in at the feed store to order more grain, taking those broken bridles into the saddler and meeting with the bank manager."

"That's OK," Carli said breathlessly. "Lorene was the one who suggested this switch, remember? She's totally fine with Rick joining the team."

Just then, a familiar, tall, slim figure swung round the corner onto Main Street. It was Miss Hanson, Carli's science teacher from Springs Middle School. She also happened to be an old friend of Beth's.

"Hey, Beth. How are you doing?" The teacher's greeting was friendly enough. She was clearly in off-duty mode – blonde hair up in a ponytail, big sunglasses and jeans.

"Good, Molly, thanks." Carli's mom was all set to hurry on until the teacher spoke again.

"Listen, I was meaning to call you and ask you and Carli to come in to see me at school. Seems like we have the opportunity right now, if you have a minute."

Carli gritted her teeth and hung back.

This was so not her morning, after all!

"Sixty seconds flat," Beth agreed. "I have to go meet with my bank manager."

"Poor you!" Molly Hanson grimaced. Then she got an earnest look on her face again. "This is about Carli's work rate at school. To be honest, Beth, she's just not serious about her science. She owes me three pieces of work from this term alone. The truth is, she's falling way behind."

Beth raised her shoulders. "I hear you," she said, seemingly without surprise. "Listen, I do my best to get Carli to complete her homework on time, but at her age I don't believe I should stand behind her, watching her every move."

Hey, I'm here! Carli wanted to object. *Talk to me, why don't you?*

"For sure." Molly Hanson readily backed off from any possible argument in the street. Still, she hung on to her chance to talk to busy Beth Carroll. "But I was wondering what else occupies Carli's time.

Is she overloaded with other stuff? Does she have enough time to complete her schoolwork?"

"She has enough time if she *makes* time," Beth snapped back. "Listen, Molly, I have to go now. But I do understand what you're saying – Carli lacks motivation in science. It's the same with all her schoolwork. I say it to her father – 'If your daughter put just ten percent of the effort into her studies that she does into her beloved gymnastics, we'd have a child genius on our hands'!"

Yeah, lighten the mood, Mom. Turn me into a joke! Blushing bright red, Carli walked on ahead, away from the two women and across the street to where their Jeep was parked.

"I thought you were coming to the bank?" her mom called through the closed window when she'd finally said goodbye to Molly Hanson and caught Carli up.

"I'll wait here," Carli mouthed back. A

fear was rising up in her that was stronger than anything she'd felt before, worse than any fear of falling from the bars or the beam.

As her mom went off through the double doors of the bank, Carli slumped down in the passenger seat. She closed her eyes and tried her hardest to take in deep, even breaths – in-out, in-out. *Control the fear. Tell yourself the worst might never happen.*

CHAPTER 7

"You know something, Carli? You're no fun any more." Tanya stood beside Carli outside the round pen at the Triple X. It was late Saturday afternoon and the girls were watching the head wrangler, Ben, show half a dozen guest kids how to barrel race.

Carli tried to shrug off her friend's criticism. "Don't you start on me, please! Anyway, I did tell you about the Miss Hanson incident, right after Mom and me had got back home and my dad had given me a hard time about the whole school thing. I warned you not to visit if you were looking for an F-U-N afternoon!"

"True," Tanya agreed. "Hey, Miss H was

pretty mean, talking about school stuff off duty in broad daylight. Don't she and your mom go way back? Didn't they go to junior school together or something?"

"So?" Carli sighed and watched a geeky, city-slicker kid race Gunsmoke between the lined-up barrels in super-fast time. "Good job, Gunsmoke!" she called to the paint horse.

Tanya turned her back on the fun and games to lean against the high rails. "So, that's not the issue. What I'm saying is, why don't you lighten up now and come along to Gina's sleepover like we planned? Pretty soon my mom will be here to pick me up. All you've got to do is pack an overnight bag. Come on – why not?"

"Because!"

"What kind of reason is that? Come on, Carli, what's with the frowns and the sighs? It's not just Miss Hanson, is it?"

"Yeah, it is – I'm grounded because of her," Carli explained. "Mom told Dad about it and he said no more social stuff until I've caught up my science work. I have to get a B by the end of this semester."

"That's tough," Tanya tutted. "So no sleepover?"

"No sleepover and no fun for me, thanks." Carli spotted Tanya's mother's car making its way down the winding track that led to the ranch house. "Tell Gina I'm real sorry."

"OK, I'm out of here!" Tanya saw the cloud of dust raised by the car tyres and looked relieved. She waved goodbye and ran to meet her mom.

"And the best time in the barrel race is by Tommy Woodman on Gunsmoke at one minute, eleven seconds!" Ben yelled in the style of a major rodeo announcer. "Second best time was Macey Ingells on Columbine at one minute, twenty-six seconds . . . "

No, actually, it's not just the Miss Hanson stuff, Carli thought as Tanya jumped into the car. She saw the red brake lights wink as Tanya's mom reversed then drove quickly back up the hill. *The problem is like a smoking volcano, about to blow.*

The next morning, straight after Carli had schooled Diamond, she went to find Ben in the tackroom.

"Hey, Carli, you're up early," he commented. "What can I do for you today?"

"Can you give me a ride into town and back again after you've finished at church?" she asked. The sooner they left, the less chance her parents would have to question her about where she was headed.

Anyway, as far as she was concerned, training with Rick didn't come into the fun bracket, and so she was free to go.

Except this was Sunday and an extra session, and so she should really have checked it out with her mom.

Except again, the answer would have been a great big "no", so why risk the question?

Quit the navel-gazing and just do it! she told herself impatiently.

"Sure I can," Ben told her, going outside and getting into his car. "Jump in."

"OK, the vault is a discipline where you only get the one shot." Rick had been joined in the cool, empty gym by Lorene, who stood to one side as usual as he drilled Carli.

Nodding and looking apprehensively towards the apparatus, Carli thought that for some reason today the table looked far higher and wider than usual.

"You have a 25-step run-up plus a single second to show what you can do," Rick reminded her. "It's about body alignment, shape, quick repulsion. Bang, and you're done!"

"Are you OK with that?" Lorene checked with Carli.

Again she nodded. *The table's not higher,*

stupid! she told herself. *It's the same size it always was.*

But she was small and slight; she didn't have as much muscle as some older gymnasts. Then again, look at Nadia Comaneci when she scored those perfect 10s! She was tiny and skinny. Like a small bird – light and airborne.

OK! Carli drew herself up as tall as she could. She prepared for her run-up.

"Success in any sport is five percent talent and eighty percent sweat and tears." This had been Rick's parting shot at the end of the special Sunday morning session, and Lorene had agreed.

"What's the other fifteen percent?" Carli had asked, picking up on his faulty maths.

"Science," Rick explained. "Technical stuff to do with building the groups of muscles you need for each separate event. Eating the right diet. A little bit of physics, a whole heap of anatomical study."

He was starting to sound way too serious for Carli's liking.

"Don't worry about it," Lorene had assured her. "That's Rick's job. All you have to do is follow the programme he lays down for you. Oh, and enjoy the feeling when you're doing the Yurchenko – coming backwards off that table in a one and a half salto and sticking your landing without shifting your feet a single inch!"

"But not yet!" Rick had cut in with a grin. "The Yurchenko comes later, Carli – when we've worked our way through the programme, been to Denver to compete and we're ready to take on the rest of the world!"

Now, as Ben's silver four-wheel-drive jolted down the winding drive back to the ranch, Carli was beginning to feel nauseous.

What's wrong with me? she wondered. *This morning I grew jittery about the vault, now I'm getting sick. What's going on?*

Once Ben had parked up by the tackroom, Carli climbed out on shaky legs. *This is really getting to me,* she thought. *I'm still hearing Rick's voice inside my head – "Twenty-five steps, then bang! Round-off entry onto the beatboard, back handspring onto the table . . ." I'm obsessing over every little detail and it's driving me crazy!*

Out in the round pen, Lee was working with Diamond. He had her saddle on and was testing his weight in the stirrups as the colt sidled skittishly across the pen. When Lee spotted Ben and Carli, he slid to the ground and led the colt towards them. "Boss's orders," he explained. "Mr Carroll wants to speed things up and get Diamond out on the trails by the beginning of the summer season."

Carli reached up and stroked between Diamond's eyes. "Did my dad ask where I was?"

Lee nodded. "I said I thought you'd taken a ride into town with Ben for extra coaching."

"Carli's real keen on her gymnastics," Ben commented. "Hey Lee, I didn't know your dad was coaching her now, alongside Lorene."

The young wrangler nodded then strode off, leading the colt.

"What did I say?" Ben wondered, turning to Carli. "I got that right, didn't I? That was Rick Scottsdale I saw you with, coming out of the gym?"

Still the volcano didn't erupt.

Carli got through the weekend and into Monday without the drama she was expecting – the "How could you go behind our backs?" stuff, and the big show-down about school versus gymnastics.

"The more work you put in, the more reward you get out," Rick told her at the Monday after-school session. They were working through the floor exercise, focusing on the three connected saltos, reaching the triple twist and the high point of her routine. "You have to think of your hips as the axis of the flip – the pivot."

Carli nodded. "I see that."

"And you're tired of hearing me talk." Rick read her mood well. "You just want to *do* the stuff, not listen to a lecture."

"Right." She was happy with her floor exercise, except for one or two small points. "I was wondering if maybe I could change the level of my movements a little more – especially in the middle, slow section."

"Another relevé, maybe after the walkover?" Rick considered the idea. "Let's try it."

"The whole thing?"

He nodded. "From the beginning, one last time."

Make it good! Carli told herself. She waited for the music to lift her spirits.

Then, the second she began to move, she felt the stress of the last few days slip away. She threw herself into handsprings and leaps, dancing across the diagonal, pulling off fabulous scissor kicks, using the full extent of the mat.

Rick, watching from the side, nodded. He could tell she was really dancing, letting the music take her.

"Good job, Carli!" he called as she came to the end of the routine. He called her over. "No relevé," he reported back. "It works better without."

"OK." Winded, but happy with her performance, Carli stood with her hands on her hips.

"Listen," Rick went on. "I want us think ahead to Denver."

Carli nodded. Her new coach sounded serious and intense as usual.

"The competition is twelve days from now. The Under-16 section will bring in gymnasts from across the state."

Another nod.

"I want you to really test yourself against the best in the state – to be at the top of your game."

"I know. Me too." This face-to-face talk was bringing home the importance of the competition. Carli felt her stomach churn.

"It'll mean putting all your focus on training up until then. No late nights."

"As if!" Carli gave a hollow laugh. "That's no problem, Rick. I promise to get my beauty sleep!"

"So you're ready to give it everything?" he asked.

Carli took a deep breath, then nodded.

"Cool!" he said. "That's exactly the answer I was looking for."

When it happened, it wasn't the volcano Carli had been dreading. No explosions, no anger, only the cold decision served up to her on a plate.

"Your mom and I have been talking,"

her dad began. For once he'd picked her up from the gym himself and was driving her home. The sun was setting behind the mountains, leaving a black, jagged outline against a deep red sky.

Carli stole a quick glance at her father's face. His don't-mess-with-me expression was even more set than usual, his voice tight with controlled emotion.

"Your mom had a phone call from your principal, Karl Mitchell. He told her about the problems you've been having in school."

"I'm sorry, Dad. I am trying to catch up in science, honest!"

"I don't want to hear it, Carli. Just listen. They talked about the problems and your mom had to admit that good grades were not your priority – never have been. As she explained to him, not all kids make straight-A students."

Where was this going? Carli had expected another big fight, but this wasn't how it was working out.

"We knew from the get-go you weren't the brainy type, Carli." Her dad took the dirt track towards the ranch. Years of driving the route allowed him to go perilously close to the sheer edge without putting them in actual danger. "At three years old we could put you on a horse and know you'd stick in that saddle through thick and thin. But ask you to sit for five minutes looking at a book – no way!

"That's what your mom told Mitchell. The below-average grades don't bother us. But we do kind of feel that you're wasting a lot of time in school, including the forty-five-minute ride in and back again, when you're never going to be academically gifted. Plus, we need as much help as we can get with running the ranch."

This was a long speech from her dad. The car swerved again. *I get it!* Carli thought with a sudden lurch of her heart as they careered along.

"So your mom and I talked it through and called Mitchell back. We told him we plan to take you out of school as soon as we can, which is the end of the week."

"And then what?" Carli cried. She leaned forward and braced both arms against the dusty dashboard as the Jeep jolted and her life turned upside down.

"Then we home-school you," her dad replied calmly. "Your mom will direct your studies at the ranch from here on in. That'll be it until you're old enough to quit."

CHAPTER 8

Carli cried herself to sleep. She woke up crying.

This home-schooling stuff isn't about getting me better grades, she thought as she ate breakfast in silence and her mom and dad carried out their normal ranch chores. *For a start, how will Mom find the time to teach me properly? No, this is about making life easier for them, getting me to work more hours for them.*

The way Carli saw it, this was definitely the way it stacked up, and she cried some more as her dad drove her to school.

The second she walked into the building, Tanya noticed her eyes were red and puffy. She pulled Carli to one side.

"Time to share," she told her firmly.

Carli shook her head. "If I talk about it, I'll fall apart."

"Go ahead, fall. I'm here to pick up the pieces."

"It's so not fair." Carli's lip trembled but she held back the tears. "This should be the best time of my life. I have a new coach. He thinks I'm good enough to do well in Denver in the Under-16s competition a week on Saturday. I should be on cloud nine!"

"But?" Tanya dragged Carli into the privacy of the girls' washroom. "What's gone wrong?"

"Everything! My mom and dad – that's what went wrong!"

"I hear you. Sometimes I feel like that too – like this morning, when Dad wouldn't let me wear mascara to school. He made me wash my face and come in with it buck naked!"

Carli's strangled laugh turned into a sob.

"They're going to home-school me, starting next week," she blurted out. "I have to quit Springs Middle School this Friday."

"Oh my gosh, Carli!" Tanya grabbed her arm. "When will I see you? I mean, will you still come to gymnastics? Please say yes!"

"I don't know," Carli confessed. "I guess they haven't told me about that yet. And I'm too scared to push it."

"But you have to come. What about Rick and Lorene? They won't let you stop. You're way too talented!"

"Thanks, Tanya." Carli ran the cold tap and washed her face to get back in control. "Don't tell anyone else what I just told you, OK?"

Tanya nodded. "You know me – Tanya Velcro-Mouth!"

"Only I don't want them to gossip. I want to slide out of here on Friday without making it a big deal."

"You're shaking!" Tanya said. "Are you sure you're OK to go to class?"

"I'm cool," Carli said, holding her head high as they went out into the corridor.

Wednesday was Carli's last science class. After the lesson, she stayed behind to hand in her books.

At first Miss Hanson didn't look her in the eye. "You can leave them on the shelf," she said, turning her back. Then she re-thought her uncaring front. "Listen, Carli – I hope your parents' decision to take you out of school wasn't just down to me."

Carli had her guard up, as she'd had since her talk with Tanya two days before. "No way, Miss Hanson. My folks just think home-schooling is the way to go from now on. It's not like it's a big drama or anything."

"Fine. Only, I do realize it will take you away from your friends, you living such a long way out of town and all."

"That's OK. I'll have more time to train the colts. That's what I want to do with my life after I'm through with education." *Let me out of here before I fall apart,* Carli thought. She was putting so much effort into putting on this front that her whole body had started to shake again.

"Honestly? I heard it was gymnastics that you were into," Miss Hanson said. "Will you still be able to do that when you're being home-schooled?"

"I guess," Carli answered, as casually as she could manage. "But gymnastics doesn't last forever, does it? I mean, it's not something to hook the whole of your life on, let's face it!"

"How did Carli do today?" Lorene asked Rick after Wednesday's coaching session on the beam. Carli had rushed off to catch her ride with Ben.

"It's not her best event," he shrugged. "But this kid has iron willpower. She makes herself focus, even when she's not having a great time up there."

Lorene listened carefully. "Yeah, but however strong-willed she is, there's something different about her lately. Less 'bounce', as you call it. Did she say anything to you?"

Rick shook his head. "We worked on the routine. She did what she needed to do to prepare for Denver at the end of next week. We didn't talk."

"But something's definitely wrong," Lorene said thoughtfully. "In the past, the one thing you could rely on with Carli is that she'd dismount from the apparatus or finish her floor exercise with a grin spreading from ear to ear!"

At home, whenever she had a few minutes free from ranch chores, Carli worked on the programme of exercises that Rick had given her to build up extra upper-body strength. At school, she got through her last week with just Tanya knowing her secret. On Friday, she went out through the gates for the final time.

"I'm so going to miss you!" Tanya's feelings spilled out of her as she and Carli walked through town. "We've been going to school together since we were six years old, for Pete's sake!"

"I'll miss you too," Carli confessed. Her stomach felt tight and weird, her brain wasn't taking things in the way it should, so nothing was fitting together and making proper sense.

Was this really it? What was going to be the pattern of her life from now on?

"But I'll see you at the gym tomorrow?" Tanya asked anxiously. "Tell me you'll be there!"

Carli's head swam as she nodded and said goodbye. She still hadn't broached the subject at home. "There's Mom, waiting for me outside the bank. I have to go, Tanya. See you later – bye!"

"Did you hand over all your books?" Beth asked on the drive home.

Carli nodded.

"And you said your goodbyes? Did you thank your teachers, Carli? I hope you did. After all, this home-schooling decision has nothing to do with the quality of their teaching. They worked hard with you and I wouldn't want you to be ungrateful."

Disconnected from what her mom was saying, Carli stared out of the window as they drove past the trailer homes on the outskirts of town.

"I wrote off for the home-schooling programme appropriate to your age," Beth went on. "We should get it on Monday. I'll free up some time and we'll begin right away."

"Whatever," Carli sighed. She didn't want to talk about it – about how the Triple X would be her whole world from now on, how her future was set in stone – schoolwork way at the bottom of the list, beneath scooping poop and hauling hay bales, and maybe training colts if she was lucky and her dad was in a good mood once in a million years.

And where did gymnastics and the competition in Denver fit into that?

Beth glanced over at her silent daughter. "You know, your dad and I are convinced this is the right way to go," she insisted. "You remember Luke Coles? His folks have been home-schooling him since he was ten. They reckon it's worked out pretty well. And then there's Hayden Meakin over at Blue Mountain Ranch. She goes to college next year, and she's been home-schooled all her life up to now."

Carli closed her eyes. *Let me wake up and find out this is a bad dream!* she prayed. *Make everything go back to the way it was!*

Early next morning, Lee came knocking at the ranch-house door.

Carli opened it. She had hardly slept or eaten for two whole days. Rick's diet sheet had been shoved to the back of a bedroom drawer.

"How does your first day of freedom feel?" Lee asked. "No school for you from now on, I hear!"

"That's true," she muttered. "It feels weird."

"Hey, you want a ride into town?" the ranch-hand asked. "I have to collect the mended bridles and pick up a new pair of spurs for myself. I'll be leaving in ten minutes."

"No thanks," Carli told him. "I'm skipping gym class today. I'm sick."

"I can see that." Lee studied her pale face and red-rimmed eyes. "What's up?"

"My stomach — I don't feel good."

"Huh. I'm sorry to hear that. Did you call my dad?"

She shook her head. "Can you do it for me, please? Listen, I have to go now."

"Where?" Lee was worried. Carli was never sick. In fact, she was the healthiest kid he knew.

"Back to bed," she whispered, closing the door and dragging herself up the stairs.

"Carli, Rick Scottsdale is on the phone!" Half an hour after Lee's visit, Beth called upstairs. "I'm busy with breakfasts. Can you come down and talk to him?"

It was the last thing Carli wanted to do. She'd rather crawl under a stone and never come out, not face things, avoid everybody. But Rick was hanging on at the other end, demanding answers.

"Hey," she said weakly down the phone.

"Hey, Carli. Lee says you're sick."

"Yeah, sorry, Rick. I won't be able to make it."

"So did you call the doctor?"

"No. My stomach is upset. I'll be OK soon."

There was a pause. "So what's the real

problem?" Rick asked. "What are you holding back?"

"Nothing – really!"

Another pause. "Lee also tells me your folks took you out of school."

Deep breath. "Yeah, that's right."

Right to the point. "So how will you get into town for coaching from now on?"

Silence.

"Carli? Are you OK? We're a team – you, me and Lorene. You should've told us. Listen, we'll work this out. Don't let it get to you, OK?"

A nod of the head which Rick couldn't see. Tears began to roll down Carli's cheeks.

"Hang on in there, Carli. Let me talk with Lorene. Then, after the morning class, we'll drive out to the ranch and sit down with your folks. Do you hear me? We'll carry on coaching you, whatever happens. Just stick with it – OK?!"

CHAPTER 9

Rick's words calmed Carli. She was part of a team. She wasn't alone.

"Hey, how about getting dressed?" Her dad was passing through the house when he noticed her still in her PJs. "Ben needs help in the corral."

There was no: *Why aren't you in town getting coached?* or *Do you feel OK?*

"I'll be there," she promised, going upstairs to get changed. She even managed a mouthful of breakfast.

"Too late," Don grunted when she showed up. "The morning trail ride already left for Sawtooth Lake. Ben had his hands full, I can tell you."

Feeling the full force of her dad's put-down, Carli swept out the tackroom, watching the clock, counting the minutes until Rick and Lorene arrived.

"Lunchtime!" Beth announced just before midday.

The riders were back in the corral, tying up their horses, happy with their morning's ride.

Carli forced down a chicken sandwich, checked her watch again, then looked out for Rick's car on the steep driveway.

But the only car raising dust on the track belonged to Lee. He drove too fast and screeched to a halt outside the tackroom, ignoring Carli as she ran out to meet him.

"Lee!" she called.

But he didn't stop to talk. Instead, he strode into the bunkhouse and shut the door.

And Carli was growing edgier by the minute as another hour passed and her coaches still didn't put in an appearance.

Rick shouldn't have promised what he couldn't deliver, she grumbled to herself. *It looks like he talked to Lorene and she's not in agreement. She's telling him to let it drop – no way can they carry on coaching me if I can't get into town!*

She'd started the day at her lowest point. Rick's promise had raised her. But now she was down, flat on the floor again.

"I want to carry on in gymnastics," she told Diamond as the sorrel colt stood in the feed stall munching grain. "I *do!* Sure, it can be scary, and it's a whole heap of hard work, especially with Rick giving me a tough time over all the technical stuff. But it's what I do!"

And now she saw herself – a lithe, slim figure pounding towards the beatboard, springing onto the table, twisting through the air. She felt herself swing like a pendulum from bar to bar, releasing then catching, twisting and swinging again.

"I do it well!" she told the unconcerned

colt. "When I'm up on the bar, my balance is one hundred percent steady as a rock. When I'm doing my floor exercise, I flip and twist and fly like a bird!"

I don't want to stop, she told herself, feeling her confidence flow back to banish her blues. *I want to go to Denver, I want to compete and I want to win!*

"Carli? It's me – Lorene."

The phone call came at three o'clock that afternoon. Carli's mom had rerouted it from the house to the tackroom, where Carli took it in the tiny, chaotic office full of dusty papers and odd bits of broken tack.

"What happened?" Carli demanded. "Why didn't you and Rick come out to the ranch?"

"That's why I'm calling." Lorene sounded hesitant. "Something bad has happened."

"It's OK, no need to tell me," Carli jumped in, her heart thudding with disappointment. "You two talked and decided it was too complicated for me to carry on training. That's OK, I can handle it."

"No, Carli – listen!"

"Like I said, I can handle it. No need to explain."

"It's not like that!" Lorene insisted. "I want you just to listen. Something came up, with Rick. I still can't believe it!"

"Rick!" Carli was worried. "What happened to him? Is he OK?"

"Yeah, he's OK," Lorene assured her. "He's not hurt or sick or anything. But he's in a tight spot right now. I just went to see him and he said I should go ahead and tell you what happened."

"You went to see him where?" Carli demanded. A big black fly buzzed at the cobwebby office window, trying to escape. "What did he say you should tell me?"

"You need to sit down," Lorene warned. "OK, Carli, brace yourself – Rick's in jail.

The sheriff arrested him."

"You're kidding!" Carli gasped. "Tell me this is a joke, Lorene."

"Listen. Rick was seen driving into the gas station next to the shopping mall. It was around eleven, just after he and I had talked and decided to drive out to the Triple X. Rick said his car needed gas. He planned to fill up the tank while I finished my class. Apparently, he did this, then he went into the shop to buy a newspaper.

"Only, according to the clerk, he had no intention of paying for the paper. If you believe what the guy told the sheriff, Rick gave some wild story to distract him, reached into the cash register while his back was turned and stole around a thousand dollars. He ran off without even stopping to collect his car!"

"That doesn't make sense!" Carli protested. The trapped fly flew straight at her and she brushed it aside. "Rick wouldn't do that!"

"I know. But the clerk, even though he was new in the job, was still able to give the sheriff a description and it fitted Rick. Plus, there's the car still standing there." Lorene finished with the facts, then sighed. "If it's true and Rick truly was short of cash, why didn't he come to me? I'd have helped him out with money, no problem."

"I know, I know." Carli was still reeling. "What happens now, Lorene?"

"It looks like they have enough evidence to charge Rick with theft."

"But they can't – he wouldn't!"

"I'm sorry, Carli, but that's the way it's heading." Lorene waited for a few moments. "Listen, I can still drive out to see you if you like. I can come by myself and explain a few things to your folks."

"No," Carli muttered quickly. "No thanks, Lorene, there's no point."

"You're sure?"

"Yeah, I mean, if Rick's in jail and he's guilty, I lose my chief coach."

"I know – I'm truly sorry!"

Carli took a deep breath to steady herself. "It's OK, Lorene. And listen, I know this is a small thing compared with what Rick's going through. But without him as my coach, there's no way I'll get to Denver next week!"

Carli drifted through the rest of the warm afternoon in a dejected daze. Just before five o'clock, she bumped into Lee in the empty corral.

He stopped to lean against the barn door, head hanging, his face hidden by the brim of his Stetson and looking as if the world had come to an end.

Carli went up to him. "Did you hear the news?" she asked quietly.

Lee looked up and nodded. "Lorene called me and told me where Dad had ended up."

"I'm shocked!" Carli said.

"Yeah. I was worried about him, but

even I didn't think it would end this way."

"No, I mean that I don't believe it. There must be some mistake."

"You sound like my dad," Lee sighed. "That's what he's telling the sheriff – it's a mistake, he didn't do it, yack-yack! But from what I hear, they caught him red-handed."

"Lee, this is awful . . ."

"I'm so disappointed," the young wrangler admitted, his voice hardly more than a whisper. "I hoped this move to Colorado would be a new start for him, but now look."

"Stop!" Carli didn't want to hear. She made Lee step inside the barn where it was shaded and private. "If your dad says he's innocent, I believe him. So should you, 'cos you're his son! He never did anything like this before, did he?"

Lee shook his head. "He may have done a heap of crazy stuff, but he was never dishonest or in trouble with the law."

"So why start now?" Carli argued. "Just

when he's set to take me to competitions and turn me into the star he's always wanted to discover? You said yourself, it's what he wanted to do since way back."

"Yeah." Lee frowned. A small glimmer of hope showed in his eyes. "You know, maybe there is some mistake . . . "

"For sure! OK, so you've lost sleep over Rick," Carli admitted. "But you wouldn't be this upset if you didn't care about him, and I'm sure he cares about you. There's a lot of love there between you, even if you don't show it . . . Hey, what am I saying!"

"What is it?" Startled, Lee took Carli by the shoulder. "Come on, what's on your mind?"

"I just realized something. You — you're always thinking negative stuff about your dad. When you drove back here at midday, you were banging doors and ignoring people. Had you just run into Rick before you left town?"

"What if I had?" Lee asked. "It doesn't help with this arrest stuff. Let's try to stick with the main point here."

"But this is the main point!" Carli argued. "You two met up just before you drove home, is that right?"

"Yeah. So?"

"So what time was that – can you remember?"

"Around eleven, maybe eleven-fifteen. I ran into him on Main Street, right outside Annie's bakery, but he just about cut me dead – said he had to go and get gas, but he couldn't remember where he'd parked his car, so he had no time to talk. The same old stuff."

"And you arrived here at midday." As far as Carli could see, this all added up. "Listen, Lee, Lorene told me the robbery happened right then – right at the time when you saw your dad trying to find his car!"

Lee stared. "Are you sure?"

"Certain!" she cried, grabbing him by the

arm and pulling him into the yard. "And there will be witnesses in Annie's to back you up. Come on, Lee, we've got to go!"

"You folks can visit," the sheriff told Lee and Lorene. "So long as you don't object to my leaving this door open so I can listen in. But you stay in the office with me," he told Carli.

Lee and Carli had driven into town. Their first stop was to pick up Lorene. The second stop was the town jail.

"But I want to see Rick!" Carli protested.

"Sit!" the sheriff told her.

So she sat. She watched Lorene and Lee walk through to the next room. Through the open door she spotted iron bars making a partition between prisoners and visitors. Carli shuddered to think of Rick locked up behind them.

"OK, Rick." Lorene began without any beating about the bush. "What exactly happened this morning, after you left me to buy gas?"

"I never made it," he told her. "I walked out into the parking lot to where I left my car, but it wasn't there. For a minute or two, I thought I was going crazy."

Keeping her ears open, Carli threw a glance at the sheriff, who sat turning and tapping his pencil against the desk.

"You couldn't make this up!" the sheriff told her with a cynical wink. He was in his fifties, with a papery, wrinkled face and a worn expression that said he'd been in the job way too long.

"What next?" Lorene prompted Rick.

"I thought maybe I'd got it wrong – that I'd left my car outside my house and walked over to the gym to see you. I wasn't sure – I thought I'd had a senior moment, maybe. So I headed off down Main Street."

"Which is where you ran into me," Lee put in. "And you cut me dead."

The sheriff's pencil stopped in mid-air. His expression grew more alert.

"Right!" Rick confirmed. "But I never found my car, Lee, I swear. It wasn't outside my house, so I ran back to the gym's parking lot to double-check, and it wasn't there either."

"Could somebody have stolen it?" Lorene asked quickly. "That's what I'm figuring, Rick – that the guy who robbed the gas station stole your car first."

"Huh!" the sheriff looked like a tracker dog whose ear was pricked. "That would explain why the car was left there – to incriminate Scottsdale."

" . . . I guess that could be true," Rick told Lorene uncertainly. "The only thing I know for sure is I never drove that car into the gas station. I never stole the money!"

"And here's Lee to prove it," Lorene insisted. "Are you listening to this, Sheriff?" she yelled through the doorway. "Are you writing it all down?"

"Yeah, Dad, you were with me!" Lee declared in a loud voice. "I'm your alibi!"

CHAPTER 10

"It turns out the guy at the gas station was in on it," Lee explained to Don and Beth Carroll, back at the ranch.

News of Rick Scottsdale's arrest and subsequent release had spread like wildfire around the small town. Now, late on Saturday evening, Lee was telling his boss the full story while Carli stood impatiently in the doorway.

Outside in the yard, her two coaches sat waiting in Lorene's car, though Carli's parents didn't know yet that Lorene and Rick had come to see them.

"The clerk and the guy who actually pulled off the robbery planned it together. They set my dad up because he looked like an easy target — someone new in town, a bit of a drifter, looking like his luck was running out. They knew he didn't have too many friends around. So one guy steals his car and drives it into the gas station. The cashier gives my dad's description as the guilty party. The car is there as evidence."

"A mean trick," Don grunted. "How long did Sheriff Perry take to get the full story out of those two guys?"

"Approximately sixty seconds," Lee grinned. "They caved in the minute he knocked on their motel-room door and showed them his search warrant. The stolen cash was stashed in a bedside cabinet."

"Thank goodness," Beth sighed. "And you were the hero, Lee. Walking in and giving your dad an alibi."

"If I'm honest, that was down to Carli," he admitted. "She was the one who put the pieces together and came up with the explanation for what had happened. My dad and I really want to thank her."

My dad and I. Carli loved the sound of those little words coming from Lee's mouth.

"My dad and I owe you a lot," he'd told her on the ride out to the ranch in the setting sun. "My dad and I plan to take a vacation after the case gets to court and those guys are locked behind bars." *My dad and I.*

"So now you can leave off worrying and have a cool time with your dad," she'd told him. "Happy ending."

It had taken a crisis to make this happen, but now Carli could look at Lee's relieved, happy face as he talked about Rick, and know it had been worth it.

Beth looked like she was thinking hard, struggling with a feeling that she couldn't put into words. "How about coffee?" she said briskly as Lee finished his story.

"Can you make enough for Lorene and Rick?" Carli cut in as her mom made her way to the kitchen. "They're waiting out in the car."

"Carli, what are you thinking?" Beth's good manners kicked right in. "Why are they out there in the dark? Ask them to come in!"

"Yeah, why are they here?" Don echoed, opening the door and calling the visitors in.

Carli's heart missed a beat. *Clunk* went the car doors. Footsteps crunched across the yard.

Don shook Rick by the hand. "You must be mighty proud of your son."

"Likewise," Rick replied. "You have a fine daughter, Don. Without Carli, I'd still be behind bars!"

Enough of this proud-parent fest! Carli's jitters grew worse by the second. *Get down to business, please!*

"Lorene, come in. How do you take your coffee?" Beth asked, returning with a heavy tray. "Carli, I made you hot chocolate. Sit down, everyone. Relax."

So they sank into the best leather

couches, the lamps around the room shedding soft pools of light on the paintings of cattle round-ups on the walls and the hide rugs on the floor.

"So, Beth, we need to talk about your daughter's future," Lorene began. "At this moment, Carli has a big question mark hanging over her."

Thump-thump-thump! Carli could feel her heart pumping.

"She does?" Beth turned to Carli with mild surprise. "You do?" she asked.

Carli couldn't answer. She had to let Lorene and Rick do the talking.

"The bottom line is, Carli is an amazing gymnast," Rick told Don and Beth. "She has incredible talent – something I expect to see only once or twice in my life."

Thump-thump, quicker and quicker. Carli clenched her fists.

"Hey, Carli, that's good to hear," Don said.

"A talent like this needs careful

nurturing," Lorene insisted. "We need to work out with you how we're going to take Carli forward, which includes the basic stuff about how she gets into town for her coaching sessions now that she's no longer at Springs Middle School."

Crunch-time! Carli's heart practically burst through her ribs, it was thumping so hard.

"We didn't consider that yet," Don said slowly. "Carli, you didn't talk with us about it."

She shook her head. "You were busy and I was scared it wouldn't work out," she confessed. "My head was in a mess. Sorry."

"Don't be sorry," her dad muttered, deep in thought.

"I was wondering, when you made the decision to home-school, did you think through all the angles?' Lorene said softly.

Don glanced at Beth. "We sure didn't consider the gymnastics issue," he conceded.

"And I guess I didn't calculate exactly

how much time I'd have to spend on the teaching," Beth added. "Since I looked at the programme, I'm starting to think it's way beyond my capabilities!"

Carli looked from one to the other. At first she couldn't make sense of what she was hearing. Was this really the sound of her parents backing down?

"So you'd be happy to put Carli back in school?" Don checked with his wife.

"If you agree," Beth nodded.

"OK, that's settled. I'll call the school first thing on Monday."

"Wow!" Carli came out with that same jaded, pathetic word. Nothing else fitted the miracle that had just occurred.

"So, what's the answer to the other main question?" Lorene asked bluntly. "Does Carli get to continue with her gymnastics coaching?"

Don Carroll looked at his wife.

"You have a big, big talent, Carli!" Beth said, as the realization dawned on her that her daughter was something special. "Hey, why didn't you tell us how good you were?"

"Because she's a modest kid who doesn't go around shooting her mouth off," Don cut in quickly, turning to Carli. "That's right, isn't it? It's how we brought you up."

She nodded. "But you knew how much I live my life through gymnastics. You knew that."

Quietly her parents said yes, they did. They remembered she loved to somersault and tumble over the furniture as a little kid. They recalled how she'd spent most of her time as a five year old walking on her hands, cartwheeling on the lawn and standing on her head in the hay barn.

"So, honey, you get to continue your coaching," her dad said firmly. "We'll fit it around school and your ranch chores, no problem."

"Yesss!" Carli leaped out of her seat and punched the air. Then she sank back with an almighty sigh.

"And listen, Carli," Lorene went on, "Rick and I were talking on the way out here. We've seen enough in this last couple of weeks to know that we need to step back and let you *enjoy* what you do, not load you down with technical stuff."

"Me especially," Rick agreed. "I get too caught up in the details. I don't see the larger picture, as Lee here can tell you."

Lee gave a wry grin. "As Carli already knows," he explained to Beth and Don, "my dad is a little obsessive about his work. Always has been."

"But learning not to be," Rick assured him.

"And he's good," Lorene added. "The best coach around."

There was a pause then, as all eyes settled on Carli, everyone slowly reaching their own conclusions.

"I guess I know what it is to take work too seriously," Don admitted after a while.

"It makes you blind to the important stuff under your nose – like your family, and how much you love them."

Say that again, Dad! Carli could hardly believe her ears.

"You love them and you take them for granted," Don went on. "You expect too much."

It was Beth who cried, not Carli, though Carli felt as if sharp, icy splinters were finally melting inside her heart.

"We should be sorry, Carli," Beth sobbed. "Not you."

"Don't cry, Mom. Everything's OK," Carli whispered.

"So, Carli, you get to work hard with us *and* have fun," Lorene declared, seeing that it was time to go. She stood up and moved quickly towards the door.

"And we get ready for Denver," Rick promised. "Starting tomorrow morning, with an extra session to make up for lost time."

"Tomorrow at nine!" Carli agreed. "I'll

be there!"

"And I'll give you a ride in!" Lee, Beth and Don all chimed at once.

"What makes you happy?"

It was the most important question Rick ever asked Carli, though they were to work together on both the national and international stage for the next six years.

Wild water and snowy mountains. A red kite soaring overhead.

She drew on these images now, as she waited to begin her floor exercise, already happy with her high scores in the vault, the bars and the beam.

The sports stadium on the outskirts of Denver was the biggest she'd seen, the faces of her mom, dad and Lee small blurs in the audience on the far side of the floor.

"You've put the work in, now you show those judges what you can do," Carli's dad had told her before the final event.

Her mom had squeezed her hand and

gone tearful again.

"You go, girl," was Lee's parting shot.

Now Carli was a tiny figure in a blue and silver leotard standing under a huge, brightly lit dome. Her dark hair was tamed into a high ponytail, she held her hands by her sides, her head was high.

I'm here! she thought. *This is me – Carli Carroll. I made it!*

Her music began.

It sounded like water running over rocks, like spray splashing and sparkling in the clear air.

Carli threw her slight body into a series of handsprings. She leaped higher than ever before. Her body wave was lithe and sinuous as willow branches in the wind.

Then she changed direction, flipping and twisting across the floor with perfect rhythm and timing, waiting for the deep strains of the cello to draw her into her sequence of slow moves, like an eagle soaring, like the slow echo of voices calling down the mountain valleys.

Living each second, being in the moment, spinning, turning, twisting and sprinting into the triple twist, high in the air in a moment of pure happiness at what her body could do.

Carli waited for the judges' score. Lorene sat on one side, Rick on the other.

All the competitors started the exercise with a score of 9. The judges would make deductions for every flaw and weakness. They added value for difficulty, up to a maximum score of 10.

"Carli Carroll – we saw powerful tumbling in all directions," one judge said during their private assessment.

"Smoothly connected saltos," another noted. "And there was real personality at play."

Still in the dark, Lorene put an arm around Carli's shoulders and kept her fingers crossed.

Rick was confident. He'd put movements in the routine which gave two level "D"s and one level "E". None of the other competitors had that. But still, you could never predict how the judges might react.

At last, they punched in their numbers and the giant scoreboard lit up.

10. 10. 10 . . . Carli looked along the row.

Rick and Lorene jumped up from their seats. The audience broke into a roar of applause.

Perfect 10s!

"Congratulations, Carli," the voice on the loudspeaker announced. "A new star is born!"

Want to read more exciting sports stories?
Here's the first chapter from Donna King's
Riding High!

"Hey, Valentine, back off!" Billie Mason grinned at her horse. He was nudging her into a corner of the stable, nosing in her jacket pocket for a carrot. At 16.1 hands, he towered over her.

"I said beat it!" she insisted, ducking out of his way. "I have work to do here!"

The grey gelding turned and nudged her again as she carried on mucking out.

Joey Hicks glanced in over the stable door. "You can leave that, Billie," he called. "That's my job!"

Billie put down the broom and brushed wisps of wavy dark hair from her warm cheeks. 'I'm finished anyway,' she called back. 'No thanks to Val. He keeps on pestering me for treats!'

"Aye, well Valentine's Kiss is fat enough already, so don't give him any extra," little

Joey warned. He was an ex-National Hunt jockey – a wizened stick of a man with sunken cheeks and cropped grey hair, now working as a stable lad on Matthew Pinkerton's training and competition yard.

"Sshh!" Billie warned, reaching up and pretending to cover Val's ears. "Watch who you're calling fat!" She left the stable and followed Joey across the yard.

"Val's vain about his looks," she explained. "He takes these insults to heart."

Joey shrugged. "It's not my fault he's not competing this year," he reminded her. "All he does is laze around the place, eating and putting on weight."

"He's not fat!" Billie insisted. "Anyway, I still ride him loads!"

Joey picked up a hose and ran water into a plastic bucket. "Yes, you hack him out when you feel like it," he acknowledged. "But it's not the same as jumping him and getting him to work out in the dressage ring."

Billie frowned and watched the clear jet of water swirl into the bucket. "You don't really think he's overweight?" she checked. Across the yard, Val kicked impatiently at his stable door.

"If you don't work him hard enough, he's bound to lose condition." Joey always told it like it was. "Anyway, young Billie, why aren't you eventing this season? Valentine is far and away the best horse on the yard. It's a pity to let that talent go to waste."

It was Billie's turn to shrug. "Maybe next year," she mumbled.

"Hi, Billie." The boss of the yard, Matthew Pinkerton, came out of the office to talk to Joey. "Quite the stranger around here, aren't you?"

Billie raised her eyebrows. "How come everyone is getting at me all of a sudden?"

Luckily, her phone rang and she walked a safe distance away to answer it. "Hey, Kirsty . . . Yeah, I'm at the yard . . . No, nothing much . . . Yeah, OK, outside

Topshop . . . See you there." She slipped the phone back into her pocket and zipped up her jacket.

Val kicked the door again. *What about me?* he seemed to say. *Are we going to ride out, or what?*

Billie fussed and patted him as she passed by his door. "Not today," she told him. "Kirsty just rang. I arranged to meet her in town."

Val tossed his head and snorted. His silky white mane swished across his dappled grey neck. He stamped his feet.

"Maybe tomorrow," Billie said vaguely, giving him one last pat. She nodded a farewell to the two riders walking their horses into the yard after a morning hack. "See you, Jules. See you, Bryony."

The two girls watched her leave.

"What's happened to Billie?" Jules demanded, dismounting from her new chestnut thoroughbred, Mission Impossible, otherwise known as Missie.

Bryony didn't like to gossip about her best mate. "What do you mean?"

"Why doesn't she ride out with us like she used to? More to the point – how come she's not eventing any more?"

"Leave Billie alone," Bryony muttered as she slid to the ground. She patted her black gelding, Christopher Columbus, Christy for short, then slipped the bit from his mouth. "She's getting it in the neck from all directions – Matthew, Joey, her parents. And now you!"

"What did I say?" Jules protested as she unsaddled Missie. "Anyway, I didn't know the others were giving her a hard time."

"Well, they are," Bryony said. She watched Billie get onto her bike and cycle off along the lane. "She just needs some space to sort her head out, that's all."

Town was packed. Shoppers herded into Topshop. Billie checked her watch for the fifth time.

"Sorry I'm late!" Kirsty pushed towards her through the crowds. "I bumped into Karl Evans and his gang outside Woolworths. Do you fancy meeting up with them in Costa?"

"OK," Billie muttered. *Actually, no!* she thought. *Since Bryony's party, Karl Evans is the last person I want to hang out with!* But she didn't say anything.

"Cool. Because I said we'd see them there at half-past." Taking Billie's arm, Kirsty bustled her through the glass doors of the shop towards the jeans section. "Mum gave me money to buy some new skinnies!" she gushed.

"Cool," Billie nodded, wishing she'd got changed out of her stable-yard scruffs. But Kirsty had set the time to meet and Billie had had to dash straight there. Then Kirsty had been twenty minutes late so Billie would have had time to nip home and change after all. *Do I smell of horse?* she wondered.

Kirsty ran through the racks then tried on six pairs of jeans. "No. No. Deffo not!" She came out of the cubicle empty-handed. "Let's go," she cried.

Billie trailed after her out of Topshop, following her down the street to Costa.

I definitely smell of horse! she decided. There were traces of muck on her boots and smudges of horse snot on her jacket. "Listen, you go ahead," she said to Kirsty at the door of the coffee shop. Karl and his mates were already inside. "I need to buy a – a magazine!"

"Hey, don't leave me!" Kirsty panicked – she wasn't so in-your-face confident after all. It seemed she needed Billie for back-up.

"OK, I'll buy the magazine later." A black cloud settled over Billie as she followed Kirsty. Karl Evans would blank her. His mates would be wearing stupid grins. Yep, sure enough . . .

"Hey, Kirsty!" Karl made room for her on the seat next to him. Billie was left standing beside Henry Webb.

And soon Kirsty didn't need back-up at all. She was chatting with Karl, cosying up to him, not giving Billie another thought.

Henry was sniffing hard and grinning up at Billie. "Is that the sweet whiff of horse manure?" he asked in a loud, fake-innocent voice.

Billie was out of there in a flash, unlocking her bike from the stand outside Woolworths, heading back to the yard. She preferred the company of Valentine's Kiss any day of the week to that of annoying boys making smart remarks.

Soon she was out of town, riding up the lane towards her beloved Val, planning the route of their afternoon hack in her head.

"Billie Mason used to be a great rider," Jules said to Joey as she brushed Missie. In Joey Hicks, she'd found someone who loved a good gossip.

The groom threw a light rug over

Missie's broad back, then buckled the girth straps. "Tell me about it," he grumbled. "That girl knows how to handle herself on horseback, no doubt about it."

"So what's the big mystery?" Jules wanted to know. "Why has she given up eventing?"

Joey sniffed. "Boys?" he suggested darkly. "Maybe she found out there was more to life than tail bandages and de-worming."

"Boys?" Jules echoed. She pictured Billie's wild, wavy dark hair, her shy smile and bright hazel eyes, her lousy fashion sense. "No way!"

"It happens," Joey muttered.

"Not to Billie Mason." Jules was totally sure. There was the famous Karl Evans fumble at Bryony's party – everyone knew that he'd tried to kiss her because they'd seen Billie smack him across the face, and afterwards Karl had dissed Billie and it had been all over the school. "Maybe she lost her nerve."

"That happens too," Joey agreed. He put a headcollar on Missie, ready to lead her out for the farrier who had just arrived. "I've seen top professional jockeys take a fall and never get back in the saddle again. Something snaps inside their heads. They never get over it."

Billie cycled up the lane between tall hawthorns heavy with white blossom. Horses gazed idly over the gates. The archway above the entrance to the stables was draped with pink clematis.

"Hi, I'm back!" she whispered to Val as she propped her bike against the wall.

"Joey says Billie Mason lost her nerve," Jules reported to Bryony outside Christy's stable. "It's a mental thing."

Bryony put up a warning hand and turned away towards the tack room.

Jules followed. "I thought Billie was your best mate. Don't you want to hear Joey's theory about why she stopped competing?"

"No."

"Why not? He knows what he's talking about. He says Valentine's Kiss is the best six-year-old warmblood he's ever seen. He's got a fantastic jumping technique for cross-country and great paces for dressage – better than most thoroughbreds, according to Joey."

"I know all that," Bryony said abruptly. She hung Christy's bridle from its hook. "So what?"

"So it can't be Val who's the problem," Jules pointed out. "It's got to be Billie and whatever is going on inside her head."

Bryony faced Jules. "You're enjoying this, aren't you? One of your main rivals at the junior trials suddenly drops out of the circuit and you're grinning like the cat that got the cream."

"No, really, I'm not!"

"Yes, you are, Jules. If Billie is having a hard time for some reason, why not try a little sympathy instead of poking your nose in where it's not wanted?"

"Hey, take it easy!" Jules put up her hands in mock surrender. She followed close behind Bryony as the other girl strode out of the tack room.

Billie was just sliding back the bolt on Val's door. She heard raised voices and turned to see Jules tailing Bryony.

"What's got into you, Bryony?" Jules demanded in a voice that carried all the way across the yard.

Matthew Pinkerton was deep in conversation with the farrier. Joey Hicks was holding Missie ready for shoeing.

Jules didn't see Billie, but even if she had, she insisted later, she would still have said what she did because it was true. "All I'm saying is that Billie Mason has lost her bottle. She doesn't have the guts for three-day eventing any more. You know it, I know it and everyone who knows anything about the sport knows it too!"

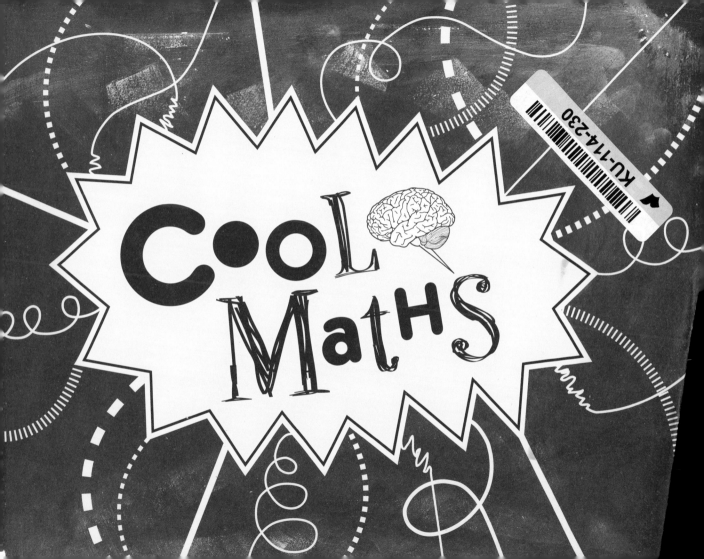

COOL MatHS

First published in the United Kingdom in 2013 by
Portico Books
10 Southcombe Street
London
W14 0RA

An imprint of Anova Books Company Ltd

ISBN 9781909396197

A CIP catalogue record for this book is available from the
British Library.

10 9 8 7 6 5 4 3 2 1

Printed and bound by 1010 Printing International Ltd, China

This book can be ordered direct from the publisher at
www.anovabooks.com

CONTENTS

Introduction

The Three Rs – Reading, Writing and Arithmetic – are the mainstay of every education system, and as such always come across as a little dull. J.K. Rowling has done her bit in recent years to make reading cooler and more fun, and has even inspired many young people to try their hand at writing, and that's great. But what about poor old arithmetic?

Well for one thing, these days no one calls it arithmetic. No one even calls it mathematics any more, it's just plain and simple maths – or if you are American, math.

Okay, maths may be plain and simple to people who are not willing to understand it, but to others it is a place where magic and wonder exists within numbers and equations, theories and formulas. It can bring the ordinary world to life in new, exciting ways and turn a humdrum situation into one of endless, impossible, improbable fun.

Yes, you did just read the words MATHS and FUN in the same paragraph, and now you've just read them in the same sentence, but how can that really be achieved? Here's how …

Maths is not just 2 + 2 = 4. Maths can help you predict the outcome of seemingly random events and the improbable. It can also allow you to find out how high Big Ben is, for example, without even measuring it. Maths can let you do the impossible and it can confound all your expectations.

Maths is everywhere. It is in everything we see, feel, know and do. It is the fundamental understanding of the importance of all types of maths, from geometry to trigonometry, calculus to probability, that has enabled man to walk on the Moon, send robots to Mars, allows technology to work back here on Earth and, most importantly, maths – and the process of computing and analyzing data – is how your brain gets you from A to B.

Leave your doubts at the door and jump into the world of *Cool Maths*.

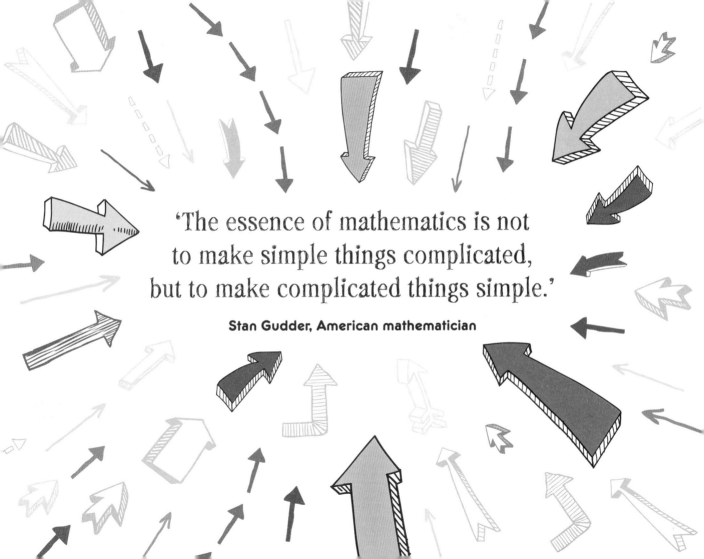

'The essence of mathematics is not to make simple things complicated, but to make complicated things simple.'

Stan Gudder, American mathematician

Great Moments in Maths

About 30000BC Palaeolithic peoples in central Europe and France record numbers on bones.

About 450BC Greeks begin to use written numerals.

263 By using a regular polygon with 192 sides Liu Hui calculates the value of π as 3.14159, correct to five decimal places.

About 3000BC The abacus is developed in the Middle East and around the Mediterranean.

About 300BC Euclid gives a systematic development of geometry in his *Elements*.

594 Decimal notation, the system on which our current notation is based, is used for numbers in India.

1950–1750BC The Babylonians (from part of present-day Iraq) know linear and quadratic equations, multiplication tables, square and cube roots.

About 240BC Archimedes produces his inventions, including the Archimedes screw, and his writings on mathematics.

About 980 French scholar Gerbert of Aurillac (later Pope Sylvester II) reintroduces the abacus into Europe. Uses Indian/Arabic numerals without a zero.

575BC Greek mathematician Thales brings Babylonian mathematical knowledge, including geometry, to Greece.

200BC Eratosthenes develops his sieve to isolate prime numbers.

About 1AD Chinese mathematician Liu Hsin uses decimal fractions.

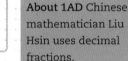

1150 Arabic numerals are introduced into Europe with Italian mathematician Gherard of Cremona's translation of Ptolemy's *Almagest*.

500BC Pythagoras and his school, the Pythagoreans, study irrational numbers, the Golden Ratio, properties of triangles and Pythagorean theorem.

1202 Italian mathematician Fibonacci writes *Liber abaci* and calculates the Fibonacci sequence.

1494 Italian mathematician Luca Pacioli publishes *Summa de arithmetica, geometria, proportioni et proportionalita*, a summary of all the mathematics known at the time.

1615 German mathematician Johannes Kepler publishes work that shows early use of calculus.

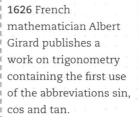

1626 French mathematician Albert Girard publishes a work on trigonometry containing the first use of the abbreviations sin, cos and tan.

1794 Frenchman Adrien-Marie Legendre publishes *Eléments de Géométrie*, an account of geometry that is a leading text for 100 years.

1799 Metric system introduced in France.

1514 Dutch mathematician Giel Vander Hoecke uses the '+' and '-' signs.

1591 Frenchman François Viète uses letters as symbols for known and unknown quantities. Descartes later uses the letters 'x' and 'y' for unknowns.

1665 English mathematician Isaac Newton discovers binomial theorem and begins work on differential calculus.

1823 Englishman Charles Babbage starts to build his 'difference engine', capable of calculating logarithms and trigonometric functions.

1976 Americans Kenneth Appel and Wolfgang Haken show that Kempe's Four Colour conjecture is true.

1557 Welsh doctor and mathematician Robert Recorde publishes *The Whetstone of Witte* that introduces '=' (the equals sign) into mathematics.

1687 Newton publishes *The Principia* or *Philosophiae naturalis principia mathematica* (*The Mathematical Principles of Natural Philosophy*).

1879 English mathematician Alfred Bray Kempe publishes his false proof of the Four Colour Theorem.

1994 English mathematician Andrew John Wiles proves Fermat's Last Theorem.

2003 Russian Grigori Perelman proves the Poincaré conjecture relating to 3-D spaces, first proposed in 1904, by Henri Poincaré.

Multiplication Made Easy

There's always someone who knows the tricks of the trade. You know, like the man who knows a good way to change a spark plug, or the guy who can reboot his washing machine when it breaks down. Multiplication is no different and here are a few little tricks to make life easier.

Multiplying by 9

Multiplying by 10 is simple: you just add a 0 at the end. If only multiplying by 9 was so easy. Well it can be. Here is a super tip for multiplying any number from 1 to 10 by 9.

Let's Work It Out!

Hold your hands in front of your face with your palms facing away and your fingers outstretched.

Starting from your left-hand side, whatever number you want to multiply by 9, bend that finger down. So if you want 4 × 9, bend the index finger (the fourth finger along) on your left hand. This leaves three fingers to the left of it, and six fingers to the right (I'm counting thumbs as fingers here).

Everything to the left of the missing finger counts as 10, everything to the right a single digit.

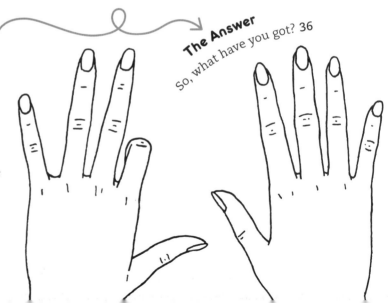

The Answer
So, what have you got? 36

Multiplying by 11

Let's Work It Out!

Multiplying by 11 often hurts the brain; it should be simple because it is just one more than ten. Well this little trick will help.

Whatever two-digit number you want to multiply by 11, add the figures together, and put them in the middle of themselves.

If they add up to anything over nine, add the first digit onto the first number and stick the remainder in the middle.

So 11 x 45 is: 4 (4+5) 5
= 495

So 11 x 29 is: 2 (2+9) 9 = 2 (11) 9
= 319

Did You Know?

When Englishman Thomas Austin moved to the state of Victoria in south-east Australia he found he couldn't hunt rabbits – the creatures were unknown in the country. So in 1859 he introduced just 12 pairs of rabbits into the local habitat. Nature (and multiplication) took its course, and soon there were so many rabbits in Victoria that two million could be killed without halting the growth of the species. The rabbits devastated native crops and altered the ecosystem of the entire continent.

The Binomial Man

Multiplying terms in algebra can look like an intimidating task, but by using the simple 'F O I L' mnemonic device you can complete the problem ... and also create a Binomial Man who smiles back at you!

Let's Work It Out!

In algebra, a binomial is an expression that consists of two terms – 'bi' meaning 'two', and 'nomial' meaning 'term' – separated by a plus or minus sign. Multiplying two binomial expressions can be similar to the multiplication of numbers. 'F-O-I-L' (First, Outside, Inside, Last) is an acronym to remember a set of rules that will help you perform this multiplication. To FOIL, as it were, you must multiply together each of the following as shown below:

As you combine the variables, draw lines to connect them, as shown in the illustration of the robot on the right – you see, he really is smiling.

When you have drawn the Binomial Man, you know you have completed all your multiplications. Now all you need to do is combine the like terms and you are done!

F = First ⟶ O = Outside ⟶ I = Inside ⟶ L = Last

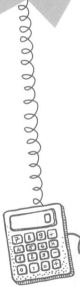

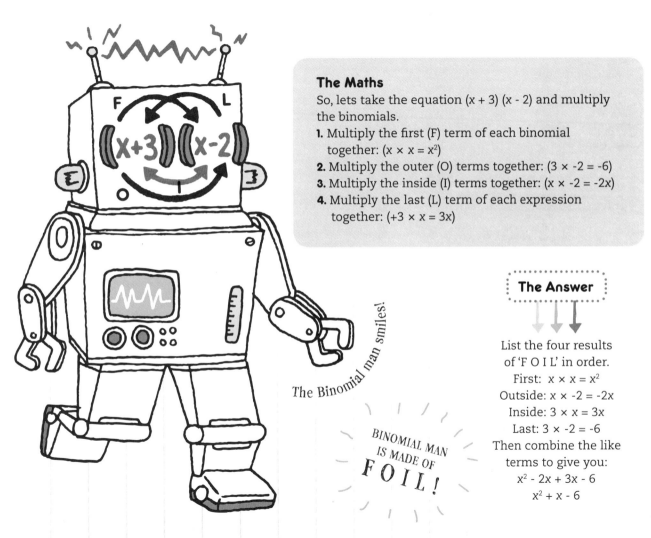

The Maths

So, lets take the equation $(x + 3)(x - 2)$ and multiply the binomials.

1. Multiply the first (F) term of each binomial together: $(x \times x = x^2)$
2. Multiply the outer (O) terms together: $(3 \times -2 = -6)$
3. Multiply the inside (I) terms together: $(x \times -2 = -2x)$
4. Multiply the last (L) term of each expression together: $(+3 \times x = 3x)$

The Binomial man smiles!

BINOMIAL MAN IS MADE OF **F O I L !**

The Answer

List the four results of 'F O I L' in order.

First: $x \times x = x^2$

Outside: $x \times -2 = -2x$

Inside: $3 \times x = 3x$

Last: $3 \times -2 = -6$

Then combine the like terms to give you:

$x^2 - 2x + 3x - 6$

$x^2 + x - 6$

Multiplying Multiples

You've mastered multiplying numbers 1 to 11, what happens when the numbers keep getting larger? Well, there's a trick for that too. With this handy formula you can start practising multiplying two digit numbers, and soon you'll be able to do it all in your head.

Let's Work It Out!

The magic formula for $ab \times cd$ is:
$(a \times c), ((a \times d) + (b \times c)), (b \times d)$.

Give the letters 'a', 'b', 'c' and 'd' to the numbers in the order they appear.
Now, how do I solve 12×23?

Step 1 $a \times c$
a (1) $\times$ c (2), which gives us:
$1 \times 2 = 2$

Step 2 $(a \times d) + (b \times c)$
a (1) $\times$ d (3) $+ b$ (2) $\times$ c (2), which gives us:
$3 + 4 = 7$

Step 3 $b \times d$
b (2) $\times$ d (3), which gives us:
$2 \times 3 = 6$

The Maths

The formula uses the same idea as a table, but just loses the zeros. Again the numbers have their place value based on the order they are written.

x	10	2	
20	200	40	240
3	30	6	+ 36
			276

Rather than writing 200, the 2 is just written in the hundreds space. Our quick method follows all the right steps but just simplifies it so you can do it in your head.

LOSE THE ZEROS!

WORK IT OUT IN YOUR HEAD

The Answer

Putting the numbers back into the formula gives us 2, 7, 6, or in other words (or numbers): 276. If any number becomes ten or bigger, starting from the right, carry the number back into the next column. For 18×19:

$a \times c$	$(a \times d) + (b \times c)$	$b \times d$
1	$9 + 8 = 17$	$8 \times 9 = 72$
1 + 2 (carried over from middle column) = 3	17 + 7 (carried over from right-hand column) = 24	2

← ← ← ←

Which gives: 342

The Trigonometry Tree

The maths of triangles, also known as trigonometry, can help you work out the height of a tree without having to climb up it with a tape measure! Once you know how to do it you can apply this nifty bit of maths, not just to trees, but to everything you see.

Let's Work It Out!

Standing at the bottom of the tree, walk away, counting your paces.

When you get 25 paces away, let's call this 25m (82ft), turn round and sit on the ground. Point your arm at the top of the tree and take a guess at the angle that your arm is at.

Let's say it is 50° – if directly up is 90° and along the floor is 0°.

By doing this you have created a right-angled triangle and because you know the length of one of the sides – and one of the angles – you can work out the height.

As we know the angle and we know the length of the Adjacent side, and we want to calculate the length of the Opposite side, the equation we need is:

$$\text{Tangent } (50°) = \text{Opposite/Adjacent} = \text{Opposite/25m (82ft)}$$

16

Most Smartphones these days have a scientific calculator. If you have one, this will give you the answer to the Tangent of 50°. Type in 50 and hit the 'TAN' button. This gives 1.19. Let's add this into the equation.

1.19 = Opp/25m (82ft)

Opp = 1.19 x 25m (82ft)

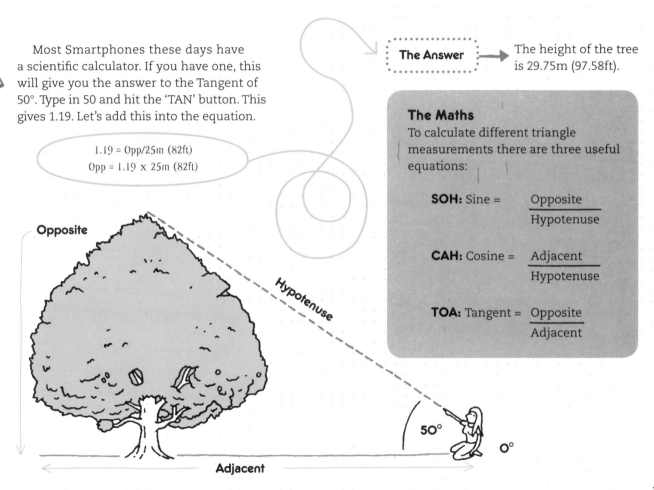

Opposite

Hypotenuse

50°

0°

Adjacent

The Answer — The height of the tree is 29.75m (97.58ft).

The Maths
To calculate different triangle measurements there are three useful equations:

SOH: Sine = $\dfrac{\text{Opposite}}{\text{Hypotenuse}}$

CAH: Cosine = $\dfrac{\text{Adjacent}}{\text{Hypotenuse}}$

TOA: Tangent = $\dfrac{\text{Opposite}}{\text{Adjacent}}$

Baby, It's Cold Outside – or Is It?

Going on a family holiday to an exotic destination? But are those temperatures in Celsius or Fahrenheit? Deciding what to pack is tricky enough already as the two units do not coincide (except when it's minus 40!). But relax, that bag will get packed, here's how to do a quick conversion.

Let's Work It Out!

So, how do I convert a temperature in Celsius to Fahrenheit? For example, what is 24°C in Fahrenheit?

Step 1
Multiply the °C by 1.8:
$24 \times 1.8 = 43.2$
OR
Divide by 5 and multiply by 9:
$24 \div 5 = 4.8$
$4.8 \times 9 = 43.2$

Step 2 Add 32 to the answer from Step 1.

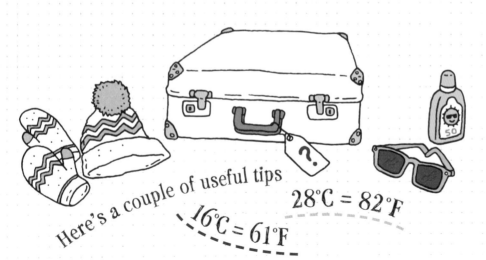

Here's a couple of useful tips

28°C = 82°F

16°C = 61°F

The Maths

The Fahrenheit scale was proposed in 1724 by German physicist Daniel Gabriel Fahrenheit (who also invented the mercury thermometer), and is based on a zero value representing the freezing point of brine. Between 1743 and 1954, the Celsius (or Centigrade) scale used the freezing and boiling point of water as its basis. Although scientists have since altered this definition, it has remained the temperature scale of the metric system, and coincides at intervals with the Kelvin scale, the measure for temperature in the International System of Units. As they were unrelated on their formations, there is little correlation between Celsius and Fahrenheit – apart from the fact they are equal at -40° – hence the need for a handy conversion method.

Did You Know?

The hottest temperature ever recorded on Earth is 56.7°C (134°F), recorded in Death Valley, California, USA, on 10 July 1913. It was previously thought to have been 58°C (136.4°F) recorded in El Azizia, Libya, in 1922, but this has since been disputed following a review by the World Meteorological Organization.

The Answer ⟶ 43.2° + 32 = 75.2°F

To do this in reverse (convert °F to °C), take away 32, and then divide by 1.8. (If you are just looking for a quick approximation, you can always use 2 instead of 1.8.) Or, once you have subtracted 32, divide by 9 and multiply by 5.

Who Turned the Lights Out?

Each planet in our solar system orbits the Sun due to gravity, and in turn most planets have moons in orbit around them. But with all of these huge celestial bodies moving across the sky, how can it be that the Earth's tiny Moon is able to cover the Sun and cause a solar eclipse? Here's how ...

Let's Work It Out!

A solar eclipse occurs when the Moon comes between the Earth and Sun while revolving, and blocks the Sun partially or fully. It occurs only at new moon and stops the light of the Sun from reaching the Earth. In fact, the Moon and the Sun are in conjunction as seen from Earth, so the Sun is completely invisible. The Moon does not have its own light because it relies on the Sun's light reflected by Earth, so the skies become dark during an eclipse. The time that the Sun is completely covered by the Moon is called totality.

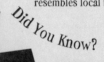

A total solar eclipse is not noticeable until the Sun is more than 90% covered by the Moon, while at 99% coverage, daytime lighting resembles local twilight.

Did You Know?

THE SUN IS 400 TIMES LARGER THAN THE MOON!

The longest duration for a total solar eclipse is 7½ minutes.

Total solar eclipses happen about once every 1½ years.

Local temperatures often drop 3°C (5°F) or more near totality.

150,000,000km

375,000km

The Maths

The diameter of the Sun is approximately 1,391,000km (864,327 miles), and the diameter of the Moon is 3,475km (2,159 miles). If we divide the diameter of the Sun by the diameter of the Moon, the answer is roughly 400. So, in effect, the Sun is about 400 times larger than the Moon.

Now let's look at distance. The Earth is approximately 150,000,000km (93,205,679 miles) from the Sun, while the Moon is about 375,000km (233,014 miles) away from the Earth. If we divide the distances in the same way, we find that the Sun is 400 times further away from the Earth as the Moon.

The Answer

As a result, the Sun and Moon both appear to be similar in size, and the Moon can block out the Sun.

Mystery Angles

A triangle is the only shape you can make using three straight lines. Basic facts about this three-sided wonder have been around roughly since 300BC. Maybe that is why maths teachers around the globe expect us to be able to calculate unknown angles, as we have had over 2,300 years of practice!

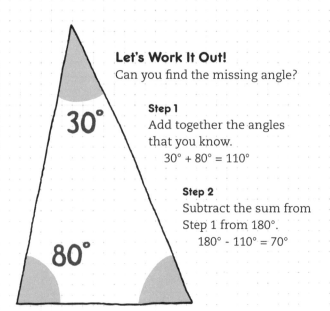

Let's Work It Out!
Can you find the missing angle?

Step 1
Add together the angles that you know.
30° + 80° = 110°

Step 2
Subtract the sum from Step 1 from 180°.
180° - 110° = 70°

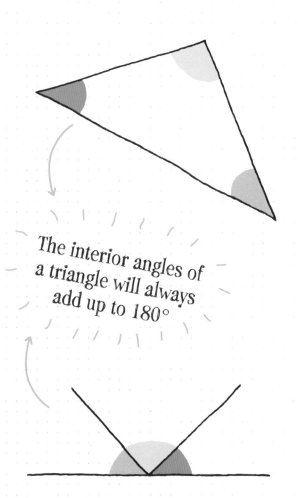

The interior angles of a triangle will always add up to 180°

The Maths

The interior angles of a triangle will always add up to 180°. Try it for yourself! Cut out a paper triangle and tear off all three corners. Put the points together and line up the edges, and you will see the paper edge will make a straight line – and the angles in a straight line add up to 180°.

There are three names given to triangles that tell us how many sides or angles are equal: there can be three, two or no equal sides/angles.

The Answer
There you have it – the missing angle is 70°.

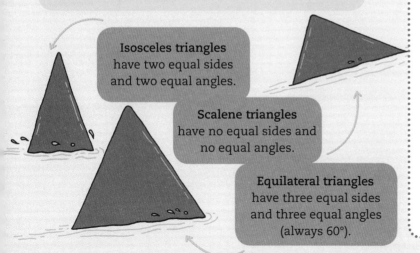

Isosceles triangles have two equal sides and two equal angles.

Scalene triangles have no equal sides and no equal angles.

Equilateral triangles have three equal sides and three equal angles (always 60°).

Did You Know?

Perhaps the most famous triangle is the Bermuda or Devil's Triangle, an area of the North Atlantic Ocean made by joining points in Bermuda, Puerto Rico and Miami, Florida. Since the early 20th century the area has seen numerous mysterious disappearances of aircraft and seagoing vessels, such as the Douglas DC-3 aircraft and its 32 passengers and crew that went missing in 1948, or USS CYCLOPS and its crew of 309 that vanished after leaving Barbados in 1918. Could it be paranormal activity? Aliens? Atlantis? Or maybe just plain old bad weather and human error are to blame. Your guess is as good as mine.

Happy Birthday Probability

How likely is it for you and a friend to share a birthday? The answer is more likely than you might expect. In fact, what has become known as 'the birthday problem' shows that the chance of sharing a birthday with someone in a group as small as the players on a football pitch, is definitely more likely than not.

Let's Work It Out!

In the real world events cannot be predicted with complete certainty. The best we can do is say how likely they are to happen using the idea of probability.

The coin toss is an obvious example. When a coin is tossed there are two possible outcomes: heads or tails. The probability of the coin landing on either heads or tails is 1 in 2.

Now let's think bigger: what is the probability that two people playing in a football match (two teams of eleven plus the referee) share the same birthday?

Let's imagine the referee trots out on to the pitch. He's on his own. Then the captain of the home team comes out. What is the probability that these two players do not have the same birthday?

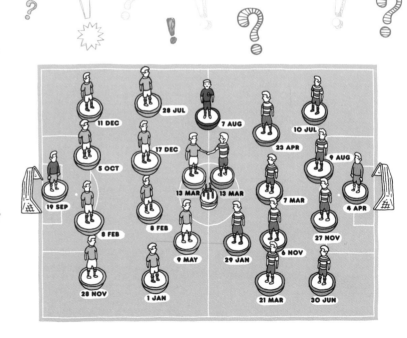

The Maths

Regardless of what day the referee's birthday is, the captain's could be on any of the remaining 364 days. So the probability of them not matching is: $^{364}/_{365}$ or, in percentage terms, a 99.72% probability that they do not share the same birthday.

When the goalkeeper comes out his birthday could fall on any of the other 363 days, so to get the probability so far we need to multiply these together to give us a $(^{364}/_{365} \times {}^{363}/_{365}) \times {}^{100}/_1 = 99.17\%$ probability that none of these three players have the same birthday.

When everyone else comes out, if we calculate in the same way as before and keep going until all 23 players are on the pitch, the last probability will be $^{343}/_{365}$.

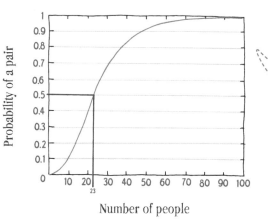

Probability of a pair

Number of people

The probability of two people sharing the same birthday!

The Answer

To allow all these maths-loving football fans to watch the game instead of tapping away at their calculators, the probability that no one on the pitch shares the same birthday is:

$$(^{364}/_{365} \times {}^{363}/_{365} \times {}^{362}/_{365} \times \ldots {}^{343}/_{365}) \times {}^{100}/_1 = 49.27\%$$

And due to the laws of probability, the probability that two players do share the same birthday is

$$100 - 49.27 = 50.73\%.$$

What a result!

How to Tip!

All around the world, tipping for good service in restaurants is the norm ... and it is something a lot of people don't know how to work out. So, let's work it out! Using this handy tip you will now be able to work out that extra **15%** without getting in a muddle.

Let's Work It Out!
What is the tip on a £55.00 bill?

Step 1
Find 10% of the total amount. To do this mentally, just move the decimal one digit to the left:
10% of £55.00 = £5.50

Step 2 Take 10% and divide it by 2 to find 5%, or take your answer from Step 1 and halve it.
5% of £55.00
= 10% of £55.00 divided by 2 = £2.75

Step 3 Add 10% and 5% together to make 15%, the value of your tip.

FIND 15% OF THE FINAL AMOUNT

15% **10%** **5%**

HOW'S THAT FOR A HOT TIP?

The Answer

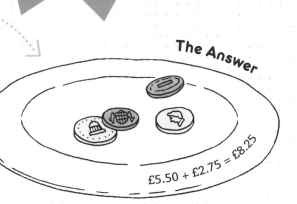

£5.50 + £2.75 = £8.25

The Maths
When using percentages, your total amount is always equal to 100%. To find 10%, you need to divide your value for 100% by 10, which can be done by shifting the decimal. You can find 1% by dividing your original total by 100, or shifting the decimal two spots to the left. Once you have 10% and 1%, you can calculate any percent of the total, like 27% or 62% or 78% …

Thunderbolt and Lightning, Very, Very Frightening

We have all been there, home alone when a storm approaches. Bright lightning fills the sky, and then we hear it – a huge crack of thunder. Then we start to wonder, how close was that? Is the storm coming nearer or moving further away? Luckily maths is at hand and can answer our question and take our minds off the storm at the same time.

Let's Work It Out!

How can you tell how far away a lightning strike was?

Step 1 Straight after seeing a flash of lightning, time (in seconds) how long it takes before you hear the thunder.

Step 2 Divide the time by three to calculate the distance away in kilometers (five to calculate the distance away in miles).

Okay, so the lightning flashes and you start to count in seconds, you get to ten before the thunder arrives.

The Answer

10 ÷ 3 for km (÷ 5 for miles) = 3km (2 miles)

1 - 2 - 3 - 4 - 5

To give seconds their correct length you need to allow an extra beat between each number, some people say 'Mississippi' in between, while others say 'thousand' or 'elephant'.

The Maths
The lightning you see is moving at the speed of light. Light is very fast, covering 299,792km (186,282 miles) per second. That will make the thunder seem to travel at a snail's pace, as it only travels at 1,236km (768 miles) per hour. You will see the lightning as it strikes, but thunder on the other hand has a slight delay. If we take the 1,236km (768 miles) per hour and divide by 60, we can calculate that sound moves 21km (13 miles) per minute. Dividing by 60 again, we get 0.32 km (0.2 miles) per second, and this tells us that every 3 (5) seconds is about a kilometer (mile). 1,236km (768 miles) per hour × $\frac{1}{60}$ × $\frac{1}{60}$ = 0.32km (0.2 miles) per second.

Did You Know?
Roy Cleveland Sullivan was a US park ranger in Shenandoah National Park in Virginia. Between 1942 and 1977, Sullivan was hit by lightning on seven different occasions and survived all of them. For this reason, he gained the nickname 'Human Lightning Conductor' or 'Human Lightning Rod'.

'Like a sudden flash of lightning, the riddle was solved. I am unable to say what was the conducting thread that connected what I previously knew with what made my success possible.'

German mathematician, Carl Friedrich Gauss (1777–1855)

Super Speedy Recipe Converter

A friend's mum has made you a delicious meal and you ask for the dessert recipe so you can make it yourself. The problem? Her recipe is for 12 and there are only going to be eight at your family dinner. You have two choices: 1. eat the dessert every day until it is gone, or 2. adjust the recipe. You decide on option 2, after all, who doesn't like a bit of fraction work?

Let's Work It Out!

Step 1 Find the amount by which you want to decrease (or increase) the recipe expressed as a fraction.

To do this, make your desired amount the top number (the numerator), and the original amount the bottom number (the denominator).

$$8/12$$

Reduce these numbers to their lowest terms. Both are divisible by four, which gives:

$$8 \div 4 = 2$$
$$12 \div 4 = 3$$

So in this case you want to make ⅔ of the original recipe.

Step 2 Multiply all the volumes and amounts in the recipe by your fraction; this can be done by multiplying by the numerator, and then dividing by the denominator.

The Answer
So if the recipe says 200g flour: 200g × ⅔ = 200 × ⅔ = 400/3 = 133.333g. Then complete for all ingredients. Watch the cooking times though, as there is not an exact calculation for that!

BON APPETIT!

The Maths
Fractions split a 'whole' into parts, with the denominator representing the total number of parts.

For example, I can order one pizza, but when it arrives it is split into six parts. Together, these parts make one pizza. The numerator stands for the number of parts you want.

Here you want to split the recipe into three parts (divide by three), and you want two of those parts (multiply by two).

COOKING IS GOOD FOR THE BRAIN

Heads or Tails?

Place your bets, ladies and gentlemen, place your bets. When a coin is flipped, which side is it going to land on? With this simple trick, it's easy to work out ...

Let's Work It Out!

How often will a flipped coin land on heads?

Step 1 Decide on the likelihood of the desired outcome.

Number of heads on a coin = 1.

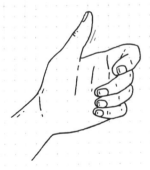

Step 2 Decide how many different outcomes there are.

There are two sides of a coin = 2 possible outcomes.

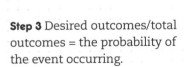

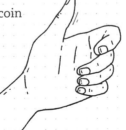

Step 3 Desired outcomes/total outcomes = the probability of the event occurring.

Place your bets! – Work it out!

DON'T FLIP OUT

UNITED STATES OF AMERICA
QUARTER DOLLAR

WORK IT OUT

The Maths

To find the probability of an event occurring, or not occurring, we simply use the formula:

$$\text{Probability} = \frac{\text{number of desired outcomes}}{\text{total number of outcomes}}$$

The answer can be written as a fraction, a decimal or as a percentage.

The 'number of desired outcomes' is asking how many positive results there are. For example, if I wanted to throw an even number on a die, I would be happy with a two, a four or a six, so there are three desired outcomes.

The 'total number of outcomes' means how many possible results are there. Once again on a normal die, I could get a one, two, three, four, five or six, so there are six possible outcomes.

So the probability of throwing an even number of a die would be:

$$^3/_6 = {}^1/_2 = 0.5 = 50\%$$

The Answer

A coin will land on heads 50% of the time, or one in two flips. Remember this is an average, so in a small sample it may appear that a coin will land on heads or tails more frequently than that, but in general, if you flipped a coin 10,000 times, it would land on each side about 5,000 times.

You're so Mean!

Working out the mean, or average, is a very useful statistical tool that can be used every day. By working out the average, we can make sure everybody gets the same fair deal and no one is short-changed.

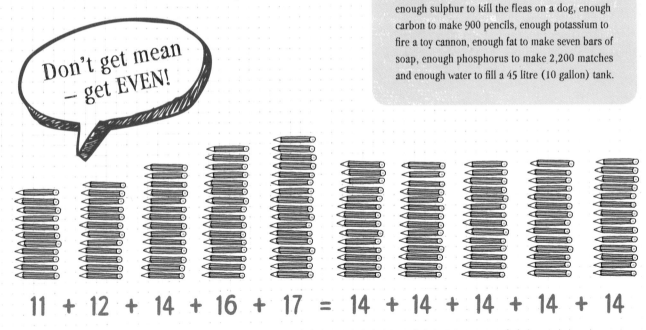

Don't get mean – get EVEN!

11 + 12 + 14 + 16 + 17 = 14 + 14 + 14 + 14 + 14

Let's Work It Out!

What is the mean of the following numbers: 11, 12, 14, 16 and 17?

Step 1 Add up all of the numbers:

$$11 + 12 + 14 + 16 + 17 = 70$$

Step 2 Divide the sum by how many numbers you added up:

$$11, 12, 14, 16, 17 = 5$$

The Maths

The mean, or average, represents a flattening or even distribution of all the numbers in a given sample. You spread the numbers out so that each group has the exact same value.

In this case I had five numbers, giving me five groups. I want each group to have the same share of 70, so I have to spread 70 out evenly between them.

This way all five groups contain the same number.

The Answer
$70 \div 5 = 14$

Vital Statistics

Statistics can often tell us which team is most likely to win the football match on Saturday or who is going to win an election. But how are these statistics figured out? It can be a complicated process, but with a good understanding of the basic principles and some common sense, it is very likely you'll be able to work out some statistics of your own.

Let's Work It Out!

In order to interpret simple statistics, we need to know a few key terms:

1. mean
2. median
3. mode
4. range
5. standard deviation.

Let's now give ourselves a group of numbers: 1, 5, 5, 6, 8. Even this small group can provide us with some statistical analysis, but how do we work it out?

1. The **mean**, or average, represents a flattening or even distribution of all the numbers in a given sample.

$$(1 + 5 + 5 + 6 + 8) \div 5 = 5$$

2. In a set of numbers arranged from lowest to highest, the median is the number exactly in the middle. In our group of five numbers, the middle number or **median** is 5.

3. **Mode** refers to the number that occurs the most often in a set of data. For that same set of data, we see that the mode is equal to 5.

4. The **range** is the difference between the highest and lowest value for a data set: the highest number is 8, the lowest number is 1, and so our range is equal to 7.

5. The **standard deviation** of a sample tells us how variable our answers were. If the standard deviation is small, it tells us that all of the numbers were close to the mean.

Hold on to your hats, this one needs a few steps:

Step 1 Calculate the mean.
We can see from above this is equal to 5.

Step 2 Figure out the difference between each number and the mean:
$$(1 - 5) = -4; (5 - 5) = 0;$$
$$(5 - 5) = 0; (6 - 5) = 1;$$
$$(8 - 5) = 3$$

Step 3 Calculate the square of each of the answers from the last step:
$$-4^2 = 16; 0^2 = 0;$$
$$0^2 = 0; 1^2 = 1; 3^2 = 9$$

Step 4 Work out the sum of the squares from Step 3:
$$16 + 0 + 0 + 1 + 9 = 26$$

Step 5 Divide the answer by the sample size (five numbers) minus one:
$$26 \div (5 - 1) = 26 \div 4 = 6.5$$

Step 6 Calculate the square root of the answer:

The Answer

$$\sqrt{6.5} = 2.55$$

So far … so what? In a normal distribution, 68% of the data should be within one standard deviation in either direction of the mean, and 95% will fall within two standard deviations, and this tool is useful in deciding how things should be distributed – examiners will use this to determine grade boundaries. It is also used in population analysis, sports, and as a measure of risk in stock market fluctuations.

I Want to be Alone ...

To the uninitiated algebra can look like hieroglyphics. But like interpreting hieroglyphs, if you dust off the letters in your equation and move them around so you can get them on their own, then you can work out what they mean.

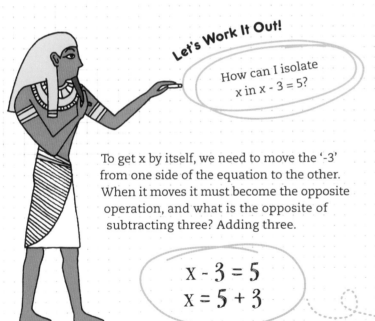

Let's Work It Out!

How can I isolate x in x - 3 = 5?

To get x by itself, we need to move the '-3' from one side of the equation to the other. When it moves it must become the opposite operation, and what is the opposite of subtracting three? Adding three.

$$x - 3 = 5$$
$$x = 5 + 3$$

The Maths

In algebra, when you want to move a letter or number from one side of the = sign to another, you have to use the opposite operation. Adding and subtracting are opposites – if I add a number and then take the same number away they have cancelled one another out. The same is true for multiplying and dividing. If I divide a number by itself, it will always equal 1. Dividing or multiplying a number by 1 will always equal the same number. When you know that whatever you do to one side of an equation you have to do to the other, it is easy to solve this sort of problem.

So what about this one? How can I isolate x in $2x + 3 = 15$?

Step 1 Subtract 3 from both sides of the equation:
$2x + 3 - 3 = 15 - 3$
$2x = 12$

Step 2 Divide both sides by 2:
$2x \div 2 = 12 \div 2$
$x = 6$

Now try these:
$x - 4 = 6$
$x + 1 = 9$
$3x = 18$
$4x - 2 = 14$
$7x + 10 = 59$

For the answers see page 112.

Make sure you mind your 'X's and 'Y's

Did You Know?

The history of algebra began in ancient Egypt and Babylon, where people learned to solve linear ($ax = b$) and quadratic ($ax^2 + bx = c$) equations, as well as indeterminate equations such as $x^2 + y^2 = z^2$, whereby several unknowns are involved. The ancient Babylonians solved arbitrary quadratic equations by essentially the same procedures taught today. They also could solve some indeterminate equations.

The Answer
$x = 8$

How Fast Is He Running?

Millions of us watched Usain Bolt win the gold medal for the 100m at the London 2012 Olympic Games. Some of us know his winning time was 9.63 seconds. But how fast was he moving? Calculating speed can be a fun conversation topic, from debating the skill of football players to watching a snail in the garden. Luckily there is a simple formula that can help you find a speed in any situation.

Let's Work It Out!

Speed = distance/time

Step 1 Count in seconds/minutes how long it takes for your runner to cover a set distance.
Step 2 Estimate how many metres/kilometers (feet/miles) the distance was.
Step 3 Divide distance by time to find metres (feet) per second/minute/hour.

So at the London Olympics Usain covered 100m (328ft) in 9.63 seconds.

The Maths

Miles per hour can be tricky to estimate, as most distances we actually see will be less than a mile. But, if we know the number of feet, we can convert feet to miles. Remember that the time it takes to run a mile will be a lot of seconds, so we also need to change our time. Using fractions to represent the same value (for example 1 mile = 5,280ft), and the idea that a unit divided by itself is essentially 'cancelled out', we can take our feet per second and change to mph. So 3ft per second expressed as miles per hour is equal to: $\frac{3}{5,280} \times 3,600$ or (just over) 2 miles per hour.

The Answer

100m (328ft) ÷ 9.63 sec = 10.38m (34ft)/second

To convert to kilometers per hour, divide by 1,000 to change metres into kilometers, and then multiply by the number of seconds in an hour (60 (seconds in a minute) × 60 (minutes in an hour)).

$$^{10.38}/_{1,000} = 0.01038 \times 3,600 = 37.37\text{km per hour}$$

Usain set his World Record for the 100m in 2009 at the Athletics World Championships in Berlin, Germany, when he ran the race in 9.58 seconds. Can you work out his speed?

For the answer see page 112.

Did You Know?

- A sneeze can exceed a speed of 161km (100 miles) per hour.
- A cough can reach a speed of 97km (60 miles) per hour.
- Domestic pigs can average a top speed of 17.7km (11 miles) per hour.

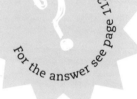

Formula, Formulae

Whether it is one or many, when it comes to rearranging a formula, we tend to make mistakes. We looked at speed on pages 40–41, but what if we now wanted to find the time it would take to travel 100km (62 miles) when travelling at 80km (50 miles) per hour? How can we take a simple formula, and rearrange it to isolate any one of the variables?

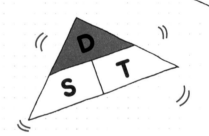

Let's Work It Out!

Let us look at our formula for speed:
speed = distance ÷ time $(s = \frac{d}{t})$.

How can I rearrange the formula for time?

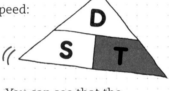

Step 1 Rewrite the formula in the shape of a triangle.
Step 2 Cover the 't' (or whichever variable you want to find).
Step 3 Read out the formula left behind.

You can see that the formula for t is:
$$t = \frac{d}{s}$$
By moving your finger over the d, you can see the formula for distance is:
$$d = s \times t$$

When the letters left are on the same line, you multiply. In this example our distance is 100km (62 miles) and our speed is 80km (50 miles) per hour.
$$t = 100\ (62) \div 80\ (50)$$

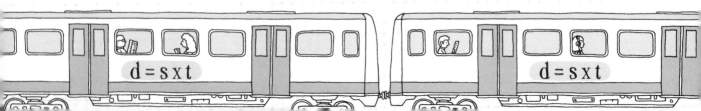

$d = s \times t$

$d = s \times t$

The Maths

To find the value of t from $s = {}^d/_t$, first you have to get the t out of the denominator position. You can do this by multiplying both sides by t, which gives us:

$$st = {}^{dt}/_t$$

We know that ${}^t/_t = 1$, and $d \times 1 = d$, so $st = d$. To get t by itself, we need to move the s. The opposite of multiplying is dividing, so we will divide both sides by s, giving us:

$$^{st}/_s = {}^d/_s$$

Knowing that ${}^s/_s = 1$ and $t \times 1 = t$, leaves us with $t = {}^d/_s$. We can go through all of these steps each time, or use the triangle method as a time-saver.

TIME IS OF THE ESSENCE!

A second used to be defined as $^1/_{86,400}$ the length of a day. However, tidal friction from the Sun and Moon increases the length of a day by three milliseconds per century, which means that in the time of the dinosaurs, the day was just 23 hours long.

Did You Know?

The Answer → → → So it will take us 1¼ hours to travel 100km (62 miles) at 80km (50 miles) per hour.

d = s x t   d = s x t

Amazing Area

You want to buy enough paint to decorate your bedroom, but don't want a cupboard full of unfinished tins when the job is done. How do you know how much to buy? Knowing how to work out the area of a room, floor or wall, is a useful skill to have – so pay attention!

Let's Work It Out!

What is the total area of wall in my dining room?

Step 1 Measure the length (or base) of the wall, from corner to corner.

Step 2 Measure the width (or height) of the same wall.

Step 3 Multiply length by width.

Step 4 Repeat for all the walls in the room.

Step 5 Add the area of all the walls together.

HOW DO YOU WORK OUT THE AREA?

$(4 \times 2) \times 2 + (5.5) \times 2$
$= (8 \times 2) + (11 \times 2)$
$= 16 + 22 = 38 \, m^2$

Area is calculated in square units!

You can also use this method to find the area of compound shapes. Break the shape down into rectangles and square to find the areas of the different sections.

For example, the shape on the right easily breaks down into a rectangle and a square.

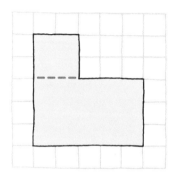

Area of the rectangle =
5cm × 3cm = 15cm²
Area of the square =
2cm × 2cm = 4cm²

Total area =
15cm² + 4cm² = 19cm²

The Maths

Area is calculated in square units, such as square metres and feet. To find how many complete square metres you have to visualize how many 1m × 1m squares you could fit on the wall; multiplication is an easy way to do this for us.

A rectangle that is 2m × 1m (6½ft × 3ft) has two 1m × 1 m squares or 2m² (6½ ft × 3ft = 19.5 one-foot squares or 19½ sq. ft). If the rectangle is 3m (10ft) × 2m (6½ft), there would be six 1m × 1m squares, or 6m² (10 × 6½ = 65 one-foot squares or 65 sq. ft). Knowing that 2m × 1m = 2m², and 3m × 2m = 6m², we can see that all you have to do is multiply length by width to find the area.

The Answer

Two of the walls of dining room measure 4m × 2m and the other two measure 5.5m × 2m. To calculate total area:

$(4 \times 2) \times 2 + (5.5 \times 2) \times 2 =$
$(8 \times 2) + (11 \times 2) = 16 + 22 =$
$38m^2$

Va Va Volume

Now we've worked in two dimensions (area, see pages 44–45) you are ready for all three. Volume is not only used every time we measure out a liquid, it also helps us figure out how much space a wardrobe will take up in the corner. Volume takes us to the third dimension; who wants to be a square when you could be cubed?

Let's Work It Out!

How do we work out the volume of this box?

Step 1 First measure the length, width and depth of the object.

Step 2 Multiply all three numbers together.

Step 3 Don't forget to add units: working in metres gives us cubic metres (m³); feet will be cubic feet (cu. ft).

3-D IS SO MUCH COOLER THAN 2-D

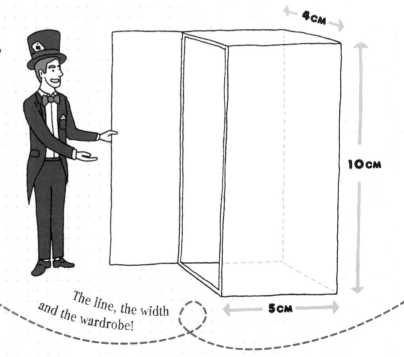

The line, the width and the wardrobe!

4CM

10CM

5CM

The Maths

In area we try to work out how many squares there are in an object; in volume we are trying to find the number of cubes.

Imagine you had an empty box and wanted to know how many identical cubes would fit inside. You could sit there and count, but if it is a big box, that could take a while! Volume refers to how much space a 3-D object takes up, and the formula of length × width × depth will answer just that.

When comparing liquids and solids remember that different units are used: liquids are measured in millilitres (ml) and litres (l) and solid shapes in centimetres (cm). It is useful to know that $1ml = 1cm^3$.

Helpful Hint

The Answer

In this example:
5cm × 4cm × 10cm
= $20cm^2$ × 10cm
= $200cm^3$

Did You Know?

Archimedes (c.287–c.212BC) is regarded by many as the greatest mathematician of antiquity. One famous story tells of how Archimedes was engaged by King Hiero II to determine whether a crown he had commissioned had been made entirely of the gold he had supplied, and not been substituted for cheaper metal. Archimedes then made a discovery while in the bath: he noticed that the more he sank into the water, the more the water rose. All he had to do was submerge the crown and measure how much water was displaced to determine its volume. The density of the crown could be obtained by dividing the mass of the crown by the volume of water displaced. Archimedes was so excited he jumped out of the bath and ran naked through the streets shouting 'Eureka!'

Going Round in Circles

These days it seems we spend a great deal of time running round in circles, but just how much energy are we wasting? How far is the distance round a circle? Circles are lines that have been bent around until the ends join up. Working out the properties of circles always makes me hungry because many of the calculations involve the use of pi (π).

Let's Work It Out!

How do I find the distance around a circle? In maths, this distance has a name – the circumference.

The life of pi = 3.14159265359 ...

Step 1 Find the diameter of the circle. The diameter is the distance straight across and passing through the centre of the circle. It can also be described as two times the radius, with the radius being the distance from the centre to the edge of the circle.

Step 2 Multiply by π; if you do not have a calculator you can use 3.14.

So let's try and work out the circumference of a circle with a diameter of 38cm (15in).

The Maths

As circles do not have any straight lines, they require a constant, π or pi. If you were to try to find the area, you would find that you could not fit squares perfectly into the shape, and even estimating becomes difficult as a circle's rounded edges make it impossible to tell the exact boundaries. It all goes back, once again, to Archimedes (see page 47). He found an upper and lower boundary for π, and by the 17th century 35 decimal places had been calculated. Currently, the number of digits for π continues to grow; we cannot be expected to memorize them all, but most calculators have a button that stores enough numbers for us.

The Answer

Circumference = 38cm (15in) × π = 119cm (47in)

This can also be expressed as 2πr where r = radius.

Have you ever noticed that when athletes line up to run the 400m they are always staggered at the start? The closer the lanes are to the edge of the track the further the athletes in those lanes have to run, so mathematicians need to determine the exact distance of each lane. By calculating the circumference of the semi-circles and adding these to the straight section of the track, they can adjust the starting lines to make the race fair.

Did You Know?

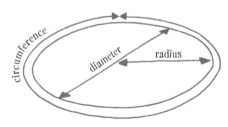

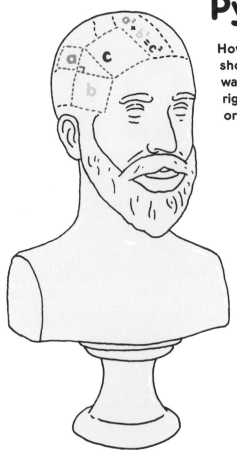

Pythagor-who?

How long a ladder do I need to reach to my roof? How much shorter would my journey be if I cut through the park rather than walking around it? Every day we encounter problems that involve right-angled triangles, and thankfully we have Pythagorean Theorem or Pythagoras' Theory to help us answer these questions.

Let's Work It Out!

Pythagorean Theorem is based on the idea that if you have a right-angled triangle and you made a square on each of the three sides, the biggest square would have the same area as the other two squares put together. This can be expressed as:

Where c is the longest side of the triangle and a and b are the other two sides.

Knowing this to be true, if we know the lengths of two sides of a right-angled triangle, we can find the length of the missing one. The longest side of a right-angled triangle is called the **hypotenuse**.

$$a^2 + b^2 = c^2$$

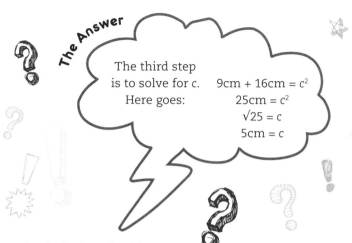

The third step is to solve for c. Here goes:

$$9cm + 16cm = c^2$$
$$25cm = c^2$$
$$\sqrt{25} = c$$
$$5cm = c$$

So what is the length of the hypotenuse of a right-angled triangle with sides that measure 3cm and 4cm?

Step 1 Write out the formula: $a^2 + b^2 = c^2$

Step 2 Substitute the values for the lengths of the known sides into the formula for a and b:

$$3cm^2 + 4cm^2 = c^2$$

While this theorem is named after Greek mathematician Pythagoras (569–495BC), records show that the Babylonians, Chinese and Indians were all using the theorem up to 1,000 years before Pythagoras. What people do not know, however, is whether the theorem was discovered once or many times in different places.

Did You Know?

The Maths

The formal definition of the theorem is as follows: 'In a right-angled triangle the square of the hypotenuse is equal to the sum of the squares of the other two sides.' Referring to the diagram inside Pythagoras' head (see diagram far left), we find that:

The area of square a + area of square b = area of square c

Once we find the area of c, we can convert this into the length by calculating its square root; as most of your answers will not be whole numbers, the ($\sqrt{}$) on your calculator will do the work for you.

Shop 'Til You Drop

You are watching your favourite TV show and the adverts come on. You are just about to change channels but it's sale time and the discount on that new TV sounds amazing! But how much does it actually cost? Is it a good deal, or is it still cheaper at the other store down the road? With a little bit of practice, you can become a savvy shopper in no time!

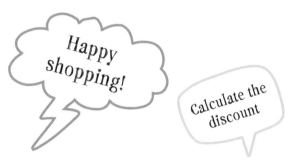

Happy shopping!

Calculate the discount

Let's Work It Out!

How do I calculate 20% off a TV that costs £500?

Step 1 Find 10% of the total price by moving the decimal point one place to the left.

10% of £500.00 = £50.00

Step 2 Double it, as 10% + 10% = 20%

£50.00 + £50.00 = £100.00

Step 3 Subtract the discount from the original price to get the sale price.

The Maths

Calculating a sale price is based around the same skill we used to calculate a tip (see pages 26–27). To do that, we worked out 5% by finding 10% and then dividing that amount by two, we then added the amount we wanted to tip on to the bill.

Here we are using the same operation: we treat the original price as 100%, and can find 10% and 1% by moving the decimal point one or two places to the left. The difference when calculating a discount is that you subtract the value from the total rather than add it on. So go on, hit the shops – there are bargains to be had and maths to be done.

The Answer

£500 - £100 = £400

What Day Is It?

Without having a calendar in front of you, it may seem an impossible task to decide on the best day for your party. This handy trick helps you work out on which day of the week a date in the future will fall: everyone loves a party on a Friday or Saturday night, but if it turns out to be a Monday, you might just end up celebrating on your own.

Did You Know?

Before the Gregorian calendar, most countries relied on the Julian calendar, which was introduced by Julius Caesar in 45BC. It was in common use until the 1500s but created an error of one day every 128 years. The Gregorian calendar was proposed by Aloysius Lilius, a physician from Naples, Italy, and was adopted by Pope Gregory XIII in accordance with the instructions from the Council of Trent (1545–63) to correct for errors in the older Julian calendar. It was decreed by Pope Gregory XIII in a papal bull on 24 February 1582. The reformed calendar was adopted later that year by a handful of countries, with other countries adopting it over the following centuries. It is now the most widely accepted civil calendar.

Let's Work It Out!

What day of the week will it be 47 days from Wednesday?

Step 1 Divide the number of days in the future by seven and list how many days are left over:

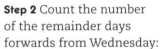

$47 \div 7 = 6$, remainder 5

Step 2 Count the number of the remainder days forwards from Wednesday:
  1 day ahead is Thursday
  2 days ahead is Friday
  3 days ahead is Saturday
  4 days ahead is Sunday
  5 days ahead is Monday.

Predict the future

The Answer
This means the day of the week 47 days ahead of Wednesday will be a Monday – not the best day for a party, but at least you can impress your friends with this amazing trick!

Amazing Trick

The Maths

The basis of this mystery uses the fact that seven days from today will be the same day of the week from which you started: seven days ahead from a Tuesday will be another Tuesday. If we take the total number of days and divide it by seven, the whole number represents how many weeks there are until we end up on the exact same day in the future. The remainder can then be used to count the relevant number of days forward.

You can use this to find past dates as well, but remember the remainder will be days before, so go backwards instead of forwards when working out the day of the week.

More practically, you can use this trick to predict what day of the week an actual event will be on. If you want to know what day of the week your next birthday is going to be on, count how many days away it is and use the same method. Make sure you remember that old saying: 'Thirty days hath September, April, June and November. February has twenty-eight alone, all the rest have thirty-one.' And don't forget about leap years!

Kaprekar's Constant

Dattaraya Ramchandra Kaprekar (1905-86) was an Indian mathematician who discovered several number constants (or cycles) during his life. No one paid a great deal of attention to his work as he was a schoolteacher rather than a scholar, but today these numbers provide us with some interesting and fun calculations.

Let's Work It Out!

Step 1 Pick any four-digit number that is made from at least two different numbers (so not 1,111 or 2,222).

Step 2 Arrange the numbers in increasing order.

Step 3 Arrange the numbers in decreasing order.

Step 4 Subtract the number from Step 2 from the number from Step 3.

Step 5 Use the number you obtain and repeat the steps above.

For example:

1. Choose number
   3,141
2. Increasing
   1,134
3. Decreasing
   4,311
4. Step 3 - Step 2
   4,311 - 1,134 =
   3,177

2. Increasing
   1,377
3. Decreasing
   7,731
4. Step 3 - Step 2
   7,731 - 1,377 =
   6,354

2. Increasing
   3,456
3. Decreasing
   6,543
4. Step 3 - Step 2
   6,543 - 3,456 =
   3,087

2. Increasing
   0378
3. Decreasing
   8,730
4. Step 3 - Step 2
   0378 - 8,730 =
   8,352

2. Increasing
   2,358
3. Decreasing
   8,532
4. Step 3 - Step 2
   8,532 - 2,358 =
   6,174

Once you have reached 6,174 and you go through the steps again you get: 7,641 - 1,467 = 6,174 And this number keeps repeating – hence the name 'constant'.

Mr Kaprekar also has a type of number named after him: a Kaprekar number for a given base is a non-negative integer, the representation of whose square in that base can be split into two parts that add up to the original number again. For instance, 45 is a Kaprekar number, because $45^2 = 2025$ and $20+25 = 45$.

The Maths

Each number in the sequence uniquely determines the next number in the sequence. Since there are only a finite number of possibilities, eventually the sequence must return to a number it hit before, leading to a cycle. So any starting number will give a sequence that eventually becomes a cycle. This also works for three-digit numbers, but this time the constant will be 495. Give it a try!

These numbers lead to a cycle

Taxonomy Fun

Taxonomy is the classification of organisms. Hold on a minute, does this sound like fun? Well not for everyone perhaps, but this trick should make you smile.

Let's Work It Out!

Step 1 Pick a number between 1 and 10.

Step 2 Multiply by 9 (For a quick way to do this see page 10.)

Step 3 Add the digits.

Step 4 Subtract 5.

Step 5 Match the number with the corresponding letter of the alphabet (1 = a, 2 = b, and so on).

Step 6 Think of a country that starts with that letter.

Step 7 Think of an animal that starts with the last letter of the country.

Step 8 Think of a colour that starts with the last letter of the animal's name.

The Answer Did you get

The home of those addictive coloured building bricks Lego, Denmark has the oldest national flag (the 'Dannebrog') and the oldest monarchy in the world, and Copenhagen is the oldest capital city in Europe. Although geographically Greenland is part of the North American continent and has its own government, it is actually part of the Kingdom of Denmark

Did You Know?

The Maths

The trick here is that the number-letter association is always 'd', no matter what number you choose. This is because any single-digit number multiplied by 9 will give an answer with the digits adding up to 9, which will lead to the answer 4, and the fourth letter of the alphabet is 'd'. Denmark is the only country in Europe that begins with the letter 'd' (the only other global options are: Djibouti, Dominica, Dominican Republic).

For those who choose Denmark, the majority of people will think of the animal 'kangaroo' for the letter 'k' because of the easy colour association of the last letter with 'orange'.

an   orange kangaroo   from Denmark?   Most people will!

Palindrome Numbers

Palindromes are words or phrases that read the same forwards as backwards, for example, 'race car', or 'A man, a plan, a canal, Panama'. You can write the letters from left to right, or right to left, and you get exactly the same thing! And you can do this with numbers too!

The Answer
And this gives us:
4. 1050 + 0501 =
1551

Let's Work It Out!
Step 1 Pick a number.

Step 2 Reverse it.

Step 3 Add the two numbers together.

Step 4 If this is not a palindrome, repeat Steps 2 and 3.

So let's try this:
1. 723
2. 327
3. 723 + 327 = 1050

This is clearly not a palindrome, so repeat Steps 2 and 3.

The Maths

In fact, about 80% of all numbers under 10,000 solve in four steps or less. About 90% solve in seven steps or less. A rare case, number 89, takes 24 steps to become a palindrome.

In fact it's been found that all numbers less than 10,000 will produce a palindrome in this way with one bizarre exception – the number 196. Although it's been taken through hundreds of thousands of reverse-and-add steps, leading to giant 80,000-digit numbers, no palindrome has yet been found. Numbers like this are called Lychrels.

Here are some more palindrome numbers:
1. 87
2. 78
3. 87 + 78 = 165
4. 165 + 561 = 726
5. 726 + 627 = 1,353
6. 1,353 + 3,531 = 4,884

1. 132
2. 231
3. 132 + 231 = 363

1. 2,346
2. 6,432
3. 2,346 + 6,432 = 8,778

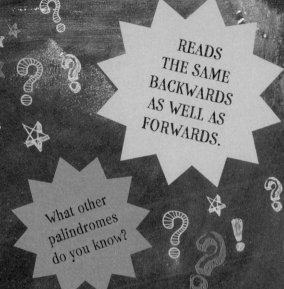

READS THE SAME BACKWARDS AS WELL AS FORWARDS.

What other palindromes do you know?

Did You Know?

Palindromes date back at least to 79AD, as one was found at Herculaneum, one of the cities buried by ash following the eruption of Mt Vesuvius in that year. This palindrome, written in Latin, is known as the Sator Square and reads: 'Sator Arepo Tenet Opera Rotas' ('The sower Arepo holds works wheels'). It is remarkable for the fact that the first letters of each word form the first word, the second letters form the second word, and so forth. Hence, it can be arranged into a word square that reads in four different ways: horizontally or vertically from either top left to bottom right or bottom right to top left.

Divisibility Rules Okay!

Division may not be your cup of tea, but don't panic as there are some simple rules that will allow you to test whether one number is divisible by another, without having to do too much maths. Now doesn't that sound better?

Let's Work It Out!

DIVIDE AND CONQUER!

	A number is divisible by:
2	If the last digit is even (0, 2, 4, 6, 8).
3	If the sum of the digits is divisible by 3.
4	If the last 2 digits are divisible by 4.
5	If the last digit is 0 or 5.
6	If the number is divisible by both 2 and 3.
7	If you double the last digit and subtract it from the rest of the number and the answer is 0, or divisible by 7.
8	If the last three digits are divisible by 8.
9	If the sum of the digits is divisible by 9.
10	If the number ends in 0.
11	If you add every second digit and then subtract the sum of the other digits and the answer is either 0 or divisible by 11.
12	If the number is divisible by both 3 and 4.

Number	Example	The Maths	The Answer
2	128 129		Yes No
3	381 217	$(3 + 8 + 1 = 12; 12 \div 3 = 4)$ $(2 + 1 + 7 = 10; 10 \div 3 = 3.33)$	Yes No
4	1,312 7,019	$(12 \div 4 = 3)$ $(19 \div 4 = 4.75)$	Yes No
5	175 809		Yes No
6	114 308	(Even; $1 + 1 + 4 = 6; 6 \div 3 = 2$) (Even; $3 + 0 + 8 = 11; 11 \div 3 = 3.66$)	Yes No
7	672 905	$(2 \times 2 = 4; 67 - 4 = 63; 63 \div 7 = 9)$ $(2 \times 5 = 10; 90 - 10 = 80; 80 \div 7 = 11.43)$	Yes No
8	109,816 216,302	$(816 \div 8 = 102)$ $(302 \div 8 = 37.75)$	Yes No
9	1,629 2,103	$(1 + 6 + 2 + 9 = 18; 1 + 8 = 9)$ $(2 + 0 + 1 + 3 = 6)$	Yes No
10	220 221		Yes No
11	1,364 25,176	$((3 + 4) - (1+6) = 0)$ $((5 + 7) - (2 + 1 + 6) = 3)$	Yes No
12	648 524	3: $6 + 4 + 8 = 18; 18 \div 3 = 6$ Yes 4: $48 \div 4 = 12$ Yes 3: $5 + 2 + 4 = 11; 11 \div 3 = 3.66$ No 4: $4 \div 4 = 1$ Yes	Yes No

Hair has the highest rate of mitosis (cell division). An average hair grows 0.3mm a day and 1cm (¼in) per month.

Did You Know?

Number Tricks 1

Number tricks are a great way to amaze your friends and family. Give these ones a try.

Trick 1

1. Think of a number less than 10.

2. Double it.

3. Add 6.

4. Halve it.

5. Subtract the original number from the answer.

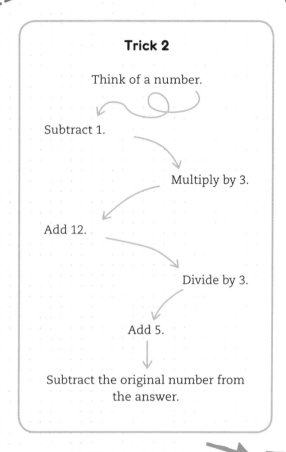

Trick 2

Think of a number.

Subtract 1.

Multiply by 3.

Add 12.

Divide by 3.

Add 5.

Subtract the original number from the answer.

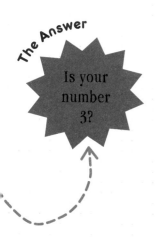
Trick 4

1. Pick two single-digit numbers.

2. Pick one of them and double it.

3. Add 5.

4. Multiply by 5.

5. Add the second number.

6. Subtract 4.

7. Subtract 21.

Trick 3

Think of a number.

Multiply it by 3.

Add 45.

Double it.

Divide by 6.

Subtract the original number from the answer.

The Answer

Is your answer the two numbers you started with?

Is your number 15?

The Answer

The Answer

Is your number 8?

Number Tricks 2

Are your friends and family amazed by your maths skills? Here are some more tricks to keep you going.

Trick 5

Write down your house number.

Multiply by 2.

Add the number of days in a week.

Multiply by 50.

Add your age.

Subtract 365 (number of days in a year).

Add 15.

Trick 6

Multiply the number of the month of your birthday by 5.

Add 7.

Multiply by 4.

Add 13.

Multiply by 5.

Add the day of your birthday.

Subtract 205.

The Answer

Is the answer the month and day of your birth?

Trick 7

1. Enter into a calculator any number that consists solely of the number nine repeated.

2. Multiply it by any number.

3. Write down the number on paper.

4. Add together the individual digits in the answer.

5. Add the answer digits together.

The Answer

Is the answer 9?

(If not ...

Trick 8

1. Choose a number from 1 to 10.

2. Double it.

3. Add 2 to the result.

4. Divide that number by 2.

5. Subtract the original number from the answer in Step 4.

The Answer

Is your answer your house number and then your age?

... keep adding the new answer digits together and eventually they will add up to 9.)

The Answer

Is the answer 1?

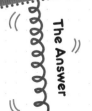

The Answer

Mind-boggling Numbers

When we first start to count the numbers are small and easy to keep track of – we use our fingers to help us. But as we get older we find that numbers get bigger and bigger and bigger. And once we become interested in astronomy some numbers are too big to comprehend. Luckily scientific notation, also known as standard form, exists in maths to help us get large numbers down to manageable proportions.

Let's Work It Out!

How can I write a number in scientific notation? For example 4,560?

Step 1 Add a decimal point after the first digit: So 4,560 becomes 4.560

Step 2 Count how many times you moved the decimal over. This will be the exponent in your final answer.
    $4.560 = 3$

Step 3 Take your number and multiply it by 10 to the exponent from Step 2; as long as you don't break any significant figures rules (see page 76), you usually do not need to include all the zeros.

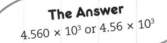

The Answer
4.560×10^3 or 4.56×10^3

The Maths

Scientific notation is a way to write really big (or small) numbers by using an exponent of the number 10.

$10^1 = 10$
$10^2 = 10 \times 10 = 100$
$10^3 = 10 \times 10 \times 10 = 1000$, and so on.

This becomes useful when you want to try to condense a large number down. Let's say your answer was 3,450,000,000. That would be the same as saying 3.45 × 1,000,000,000. And 1,000,000,000 is the same as saying 10^9, as $10 \times 10 \times 10 \times 10 \times 10 \times 10 \times 10 \times 10 \times 10 = 1{,}000{,}000{,}000$. So our answer can be written as 3.45×10^9, or 3.45 billion.

To extract a number from scientific notation, you need to move the decimal. So if the exponent is 6, move the decimal 6 places to the right, adding zeros if you run out of numbers. If the exponent is negative, you move the decimal to the left, making the number smaller.

Still boggled?

Avogadro's Number, 6.022×10^{23}, is the number or molecules in one mole of a substance. For those of you who may not be a lover of chemistry, that means there are 6.022×10^{23} individual molecules of H_2O in every 18g (⅓ oz) of water. Hope you're thirsty!

Did You Know?

It's Hip to be Square

You know what shape a square is, but what is squaring in maths? When you are asked to square a number, you multiply the number by itself. If you had a square, both the length and the width would be the same number – see how they are related?

The Answer
Now put the two numbers together, which gives you: 225.

English schoolmaster and mathematician Charles Hutton published the first table of squares up to 25,400 in the year 1781, commissioned by the Board of Longitude. After learning of the table, mathematicians and amateurs gleaned many facts from it, such as the simple observation that squares always end in the digits 0, 1, 4, 5, 6, or 9, never 2, 3, 7 or 8.

Did You Know?

Let's Work It Out!
What is 15 × 15?

Step 1 Take the first digit, and multiply it by its next highest digit:
$1 \times (1 + 1) = 1 \times (2) = 2$

Step 2 Multiply the two fives together:
$5 \times 5 = 25$

MULTIPLY THE NUMBER BY ITSELF!

The Maths

The formula we are using here is N × (N + 1). Using the same idea as when we were multiplying two-digit numbers, we know that we need to multiply our tens and ones. So for the ones, when we multiply 5 by 5 we will always get 25; if we multiply 5 by 10 we get 50, and there two of them, which added together will make 100; and when we multiply 10 by 10 we get 100 more – so we get a total of 225.

But what if we want to find the square of a number that doesn't end in 5, like 19?

Multiply the number by itself!

Step 1 Find the difference between the number you want to square and the nearest multiple of 10; for 19 the nearest boundary is up one digit to 20.

Step 2 Depending on the direction of the boundary, now count the relevant number of the digits in the other direction; for 19 we would now count one digit down to 18.

Step 3 Multiply the numbers from Steps 1 and 2 together: 20 × 18 = 360. (To do this without a calculator multiply by 10 and then double the answer.)

Step 4 Add the square of the difference from Step 1:
$1 \times 1 = 1$
$360 + 1 = 361$

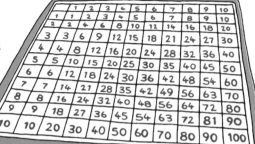

By manipulating our numbers so that we always have a multiple of ten, we simplify these problems so we can do them in our heads. Remembering too that we can break down any larger number into two or more numbers that multiply to make it as well, the question gets easier and easier.

Summation of Sums

SUM LIKE IT HOT!

Have you ever stared at your pile of change at the checkout and wondered whether you have enough money to buy the milk (that you definitely need) and the chocolate bar (that you don't)? Can you afford the ice cream and the crisps (you really don't want to have to choose)? If you learn this useful trick then you really won't need to use a calculator to work out the answer.

Let's Work It Out!

How can I solve 81 + 78?

Step 1 We want to use tens as much as possible, so round the second number to the nearest 10.
78 + 2 = 80

Step 2 Add this number to the first number:
80 + 81 = 161

Step 3 To get your answer, add or subtract the difference between the second number and the number you rounded it to.

The Pascaline was possibly the first mechanical adding device actually used for a practical purpose. It was built in 1643 by Blaise Pascal to help his father, Etienne, a tax collector, with the tedious activity of adding and subtracting large sequences of numbers. However, it was not until 1820 that French inventor and entrepreneur Charles Xavier Thomas designed, patented and manufactured the first commercially successful mechanical calculator, called the Arithmometer.

Did You Know?

The Answer
This gives you:

How about this one:
62 + 53?
62 + 50 (- 3) = 112
112 + 3 = 115

161 - 2 = 159

The Maths
Just like the multiplication trick on pages 80–81, we can rewrite any number as the combination of numbers that add or subtract to make it. So the number 7 can be written as 3 + 4, or 10 - 3, as both operations are equal to 7. When we look at two-digit numbers, we may find it easier to rewrite them as an addition or subtraction from the nearest ten, as most of us can quickly add ten onto a number. We can then finish the problem by adding or subtracting the difference. Give it a go next time you are at the corner shop.

Or this: 97 + 35?
97 + 30 (- 5) = 127
127 + 5 = 132

A HANDY LITTLE TRICK

Don't be so Negative

Now that we've mastered adding up, the next basic skill we need is taking away. However, double negatives can be confusing when you are completing a maths problem. But don't worry, this little number trick will get you feeling positive about negatives ...

Let's Work It Out!

How do I subtract a negative number, for example 6 - (-4)?

When you have two negatives, or a subtraction and a negative together, this is the same as a positive, so subtracting minus 4 is the same as adding 4:

$$6 + 4$$

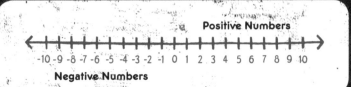

Positive Numbers

-10 -9 -8 -7 -6 -5 -4 -3 -2 -1 0 1 2 3 4 5 6 7 8 9 10

Negative Numbers

The Answer
When you add the numbers together you get:
6 + 4 = 10

BANK

OH NO, I'VE GOT A NEGATIVE BALANCE!

The Maths

In the order of operation (see pages 78–79) subtraction always comes last, so the numbers must stay where they are. Using a number line is a nice way to keep track visually.

Addition moves you towards the right, but every time you see a subtraction or a negative sign you need to change direction. When you have a basic subtraction, you turn once, so you move to the left, or down the number line, but when you have two negatives, you turn and then turn again, so back up the number line you go!

Now you know that subtracting a negative number is the same as adding, remember that adding a negative number is the same as subtracting.

So 7 + (-3)
= 4

Did You Know?

Rhesus is a protein that occurs on red blood cells. People who have the protein are known as Rhesus positive, and those without it are called Rhesus negative. The highest incidence of Rhesus negative is among the people of the Basque region that lies between France and Spain, where it is around 30%; for the rest of Europe this falls to around 16%. By contrast, among Asian and African people it affects less than 1% of the population.

Rules for Multiplying

POSITIVE × POSITIVE = POSITIVE
POSITIVE × NEGATIVE = NEGATIVE
NEGATIVE × POSITIVE = NEGATIVE
NEGATIVE × NEGATIVE = POSITIVE

Significant Figures

We all know that builders' estimates can add up – usually to extra money in their piggy banks. But when we are working something out, often we only need a rough idea. To do this we can round numbers up or down, or choose the number of decimal places we want to use. Another way to produce an estimate is to use significant figures.

Let's Work It Out!

What is the number 368,249 to three significant figures?

Step 1 For 368,249, the '3' is the most significant digit because it tells us that the number is three hundred thousand and something, but as we want three significant figures in our answer, we need to move along to the '8'.

Step 2 Now we need to look at the number that follows the '8'. As this is a '2' the rounding rules tell us that we should round down rather than up.

The rules for rounding up are:
• If the next number is 5 or more, we round up.
• If the next number is 4 or less, we do not round up.

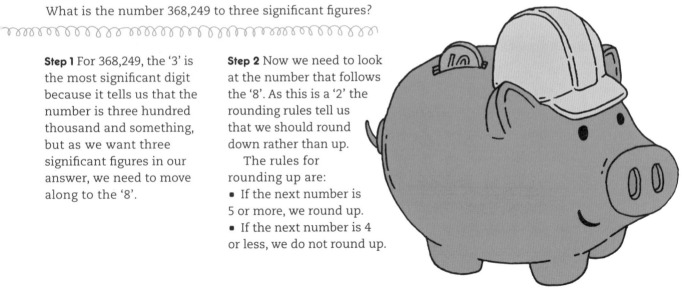

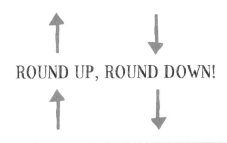

ROUND UP, ROUND DOWN!

The Maths

In maths we round off numbers to a certain number of significant figures; the most common are one, two and three.

The rules for significant figures are:

1. All non-zero numbers (1, 2, 3, 4, 5, 6, 7, 8, 9) are always significant.

2. All zeros between non-zero numbers are always significant, eg. 30,245.

3. All zeros that are simultaneously to the right of the decimal point and at the end of the number are always significant, eg. 501.040.

4. All zeros to the left of a written decimal point and are in a number greater than or equal to ten are always significant, eg. 900.06.

You can use significant figures for decimals too. For 0.0000058763, the '5' is the most significant digit, because it tells us that the number is five millionths and something. The '8' is the next most significant, and so on.

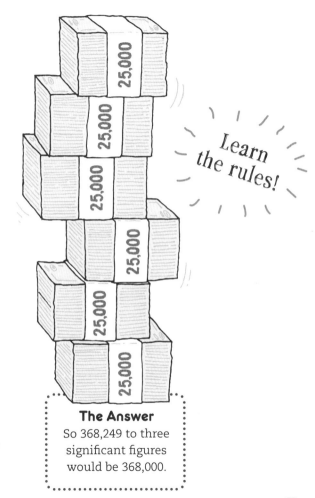

Learn the rules!

The Answer

So 368,249 to three significant figures would be 368,000.

The Order of Things

You've probably already noticed, but maths is a peculiar animal – you can do a calculation in different ways and come up with a new answer each time. Fortunately, as you might expect in maths, there is a right way to do things, and this is called the 'Order of Operations'.

Let's Work It Out!

How do I solve 4 × (3 + 4) ÷ 14 + 5?

Step 1 Complete the work in the brackets:
4 × (7) ÷ 14 + 5

Step 2 Complete all multiplication and division from left to right:
4 × 7 = 28
28 ÷ 14 + 5
28 ÷ 14 = 2
2 + 5

Step 3 The final stage is to complete all addition and subtraction from left to right.

PLEASE EXCUSE MY DEAR AUNT SALLY!

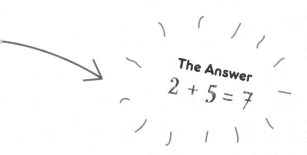

The Answer
$2 + 5 = 7$

The Maths

When solving a multi-step problem, always complete using the convention represented by the following acronym: 'PEMDAS'.

This stands for:

Parentheses (Brackets): if any portion of the question is enclosed, focus your efforts here first.

Exponents (Indices/Orders): these are the little numbers written in superscript immediately after a number. They tell you how many times to multiply a number by itself; also known as a 'power'.

Multiplication and Division: these are tied for importance, so complete any and all from left to right.

Addition and Subtraction: these should also be completed from left to right.

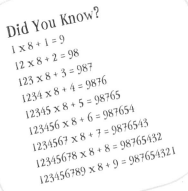

Did You Know?

$1 \times 8 + 1 = 9$
$12 \times 8 + 2 = 98$
$123 \times 8 + 3 = 987$
$1234 \times 8 + 4 = 9876$
$12345 \times 8 + 5 = 98765$
$123456 \times 8 + 6 = 987654$
$1234567 \times 8 + 7 = 9876543$
$12345678 \times 8 + 8 = 98765432$
$123456789 \times 8 + 9 = 987654321$

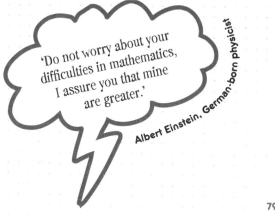

'Do not worry about your difficulties in mathematics, I assure you that mine are greater.'

Albert Einstein, German-born physicist

Helpful Hints for Multiplying

With a bit of practice, you can multiply numbers in less time than it takes to turn your phone to calculator mode. Not only will this impress your friends, you will also give your brain a workout. Practice these helpful hints to beat anyone in a multiplication showdown.

Let's Work It Out!

x 4 the number four can be broken down into 2 × 2, so if we need to multiply by four we can actually multiply by two, and then by two again. In other words, double the number, and then double it again.

x 5 Five is half of ten. If you can multiply by ten and halve it, it is the same as multiplying by five.

x 6 Multiply by three and then double it.

x 12 Double the number and add it to ten times the original.

x 14 Multiply by seven and then double it.

x 16 Multiply by eight and then double it.

x 18 Multiply by 20 (or by ten and double it), then subtract the number twice. Alternatively, times by nine and double it, now that you are an expert at your nine times tables!

The Answer
See page 112.

Test Yourself
Try to answer these questions in your head:
1. $4 \times 9 =$
2. $11 \times 8 =$
3. $6 \times 4 =$
4. $7 \times 12 =$
5. $5 \times 14 =$
6. $16 \times 9 =$
7. $3 \times 18 =$
8. $11 \times 12 =$
9. $8 \times 6 =$
10. $18 \times 9 =$

Practice makes perfect!

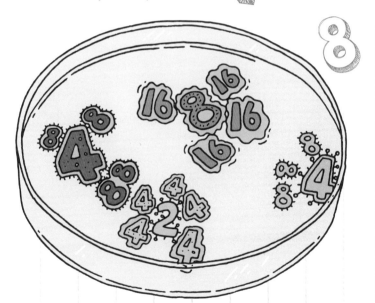

The Maths

When multiplying, the order of multiplication does not affect your final answer. This allows you to break a large number down into the smaller numbers that multiply to make it. I could break 16 into 4×4, which I can then split into $2 \times 2 \times 2 \times 2$. Instead of multiplying by 16, I can just double the number four times. Or multiply by four and then double it twice. Or, as we have just seen, times by eight and then double it – the possibilities are endless!

Breeding Like Rabbits

If you were lucky enough to be wealthy in Italy during the Middle Ages you had quite a lot of time on your hands, and in the absence of television, the Internet and other modern pastimes, people tended to do quite a lot of thinking. This was certainly the case for Leonardo Pisano Bigollo (c.1170–c.1250), also known as Fibonacci, the son of a rich merchant, who spent his time thinking about numbers.

Let's Work It Out!

Fibonacci travelled extensively and studied the Hindi–Arabic numeral system and in 1200 published a book titled *Liber Abaci*. One of the problems considered in this book involved the growth of a population of rabbits. The question he asked was:

Suppose you go to an uninhabited island with a pair of newborn rabbits (one male and one female) who mature at the age of one month, have two offspring (one male and one female) each month after that, and live forever. Each pair of rabbits matures in one month and then produces a pair of newborns at the beginning of every following month. How many pairs of rabbits will there be in a year? The solution begins as follows:

1. At the end of the first month, they mate, but there is still only one pair.

2. At the end of the second month the female produces a new pair, so now there are two pairs of rabbits in the field.

3. At the end of the third month, the original female produces a second pair, making three pairs in all in the field. This process then continued according to Fibonacci's sequence …

The Maths

Month	1	2	3	4	5	6	7	8	9	10	11	12
Pairs of rabbits	1	2	3	5	8	13	21	34	55	89	144	?

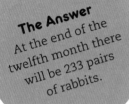

The sequence generated by the rabbit problem is called the Fibonacci Sequence and has many applications in both mathematics and in nature. Expressed as a formula the rule is:

$$X_n = X_{n-1} + X_{n-2} \ldots$$

Where:
x_n is term number 'n'
x_{n-1} is the previous term (n - 1)
x_{n-2} is the term before that (n - 2) …

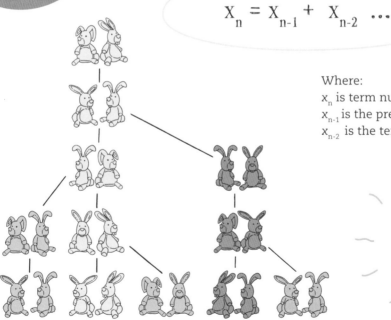

HOW MANY RABBITS ARE THERE?

In the Prime of Life

Weren't the Ancient Greeks great? They did a lot of the hard work in maths so we don't have to. Eratosthenes of Cyrene (c.276BC–c.195BC) was a Greek scholar who invented a neat way to work out prime numbers from 1 to 100.

The Maths

What Eratosthenes did was to create a simple algorithm to find the prime numbers up to a given limit. It does this by starting from each prime number and identifying all composites of that prime. As this uses a sequence of a numbers with the same difference equal to that prime this is more efficient than using trial and error to find each prime number.

'Sift the Two's and Sift the Three's,
The Sieve of Eratosthenes.
When the multiples sublime,
The numbers that remain are Prime.'

Anonymous

Eratosthenes was also a poet, an astronomer and a geographer. He was the first person to use the word 'geography' in Greek and invented the discipline of geography as we understand it.

Did You Know?

Let's Work It Out!

Prime numbers are those numbers (greater than 1) that cannot be divided by any number except themselves and one.

1. Write out the numbers from 1–100 in ten rows of ten.

2. Cross off number one, because all primes are greater than one.

3. Number two is a prime, so we can keep it, but we need to cross off the multiples of two (i.e. even numbers).

4. Number three is also a prime, so again we keep it and cross off the multiples of three.

5. The next number left is five (because four has been crossed off), so we keep it and cross off multiples of this number.

6. The final number left in the first row is number seven, so cross off its multiples.

7. You have finished; the numbers left over (coloured in white below) on your grid are prime numbers.

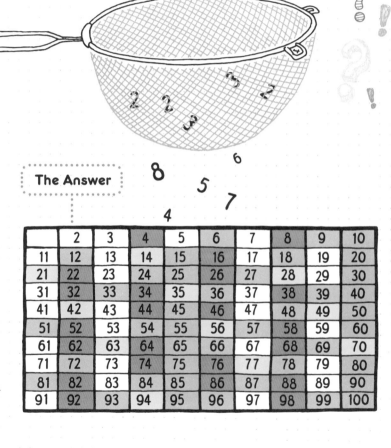

The Answer

	2	3	4	5	6	7	8	9	10
11	12	13	14	15	16	17	18	19	20
21	22	23	24	25	26	27	28	29	30
31	32	33	34	35	36	37	38	39	40
41	42	43	44	45	46	47	48	49	50
51	52	53	54	55	56	57	58	59	60
61	62	63	64	65	66	67	68	69	70
71	72	73	74	75	76	77	78	79	80
81	82	83	84	85	86	87	88	89	90
91	92	93	94	95	96	97	98	99	100

Four Colour Theorem

While we all associate maths with science, what about other subjects? One of the last areas we might think of is geography, but one problem concerning the colours used on maps kept mathematicians busy for years.

Let's Work It Out!

On a political map, each neighbouring country or state needs to be a different colour so that the map is clear. In the 19th century there was also the issue of cost: the more colours used, the more expensive the map was to print. So what was the smallest number of colours needed so that neighbouring countries or states were always different colours?

A number of mathematicians took on the challenge. In the 1850s Englishman Francis Guthrie suggested four colours were sufficient, and in 1879, London barrister Alfred Bray Kempe offered a proof that was then disproved 11 years later. The problem went on to baffle mathematicians for the next 100 years.

The Maths

In maths the Four Colour theorem states that, given any separation of a plane into contiguous regions, producing a figure called a map, no more than four colours are required to colour the regions of the map so that no two adjacent regions have the same colour. Kempe's flawed 'proof' involved the idea of an 'unavoidable set' of configurations, which derived from Leonard Euler's work on geometric figures, where countries could only have up to five neighbours. He also argued that if a map were to need five colours, then removing one country would allow that map to be simplified down to four colours. He would then reinstate that country and see if he could make the configuration work again. It was this concept of reducibility that inspired Heesch, Appel and Haken.

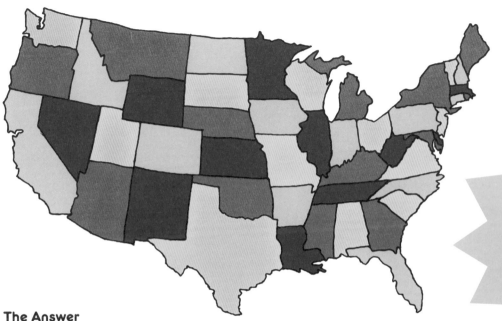

The Answer

The answer, as it turned out, was very unmathematical indeed. In the 1960s German mathematician Heinrich Heesch began to use computers to continue Kempe's work. News of this then reached two Americans, Kenneth Appel and Wolfgang Haken of the University of Illinois. They devised a computer program that tested all possible configurations and reduced them down until they could continue no further, at which point the process was abandoned and the program began again with a different configuration. And finally in June 1976, after just under 2,000 configurations and 1,000 hours of computer time, they achieved it.

The 'I's Have It!

The Romans' mathematical legacy is a curious one, that used letters rather than the Arabic numerals we are familiar with today. Its complexity is blamed by many for the fact that despite all their advances in other respects, no mathematical innovations took place during the Roman Empire and Republic, and there were no mathematicians of note.

Let's Work It Out!

How do you write the year 2013 in Roman numerals?

The Roman used a special method of expressing numbers based on the following symbols:

To write the year 2013 in Roman numerals you need to break it down into its constituent units, i.e. thousands, hundreds, tens and ones, and write it down in order:

2000 = MM
13 = XIII

The Answer

2013 = MMXIII

A particular number has four letters. Take two letters away and you have four left. Take one more letter away and you have five left. What is the word?

Did you know?

For the answer see page 112.

1	2	3	4	5	6	7	8	9
I	II	III	IV	V	VI	VII	VIII	IX

10	20	30	40	50	60	70	80	90
X	XX	XXX	XL	L	LX	LXX	LXXX	XC

100	200	300	400	500	600	700	800	900	1,000
C	CC	CCC	CD	D	DC	DCC	DCCC	CM	M

The Maths

The Roman system of numerals is based on symbols used by the Etruscans, a civilization based in north-west Italy from c.1200 until the beginning of the Roman republic in the 1st century BC.

Many believe that the numbers from 1–5 were based on the shape of the fingers: I represents one finger, II two fingers etc. and the oblique line of the V represents the thumb. The 'X' of the number ten represents two crossed thumbs. The symbols for the higher numbers – L, C, D and M – come from the modified symbols 'V' and 'X'.

The way the numbers are formed is based on addition and subtraction and these are the rules:

1. When a symbol appears after a larger symbol it is added:

VI = V + I = 5 + 1 = 6

2. But if the symbol appears before a larger symbol it is subtracted:

IX = X - I = 10 - 1 = 9

Work out your birthday in Roman numerals!

3. Don't use the same symbol more than three times in a row.

4. A bar placed on top of a letter or string of letters increases the numeral's value by 1,000 times.

XV = 15

$\overline{XV}$ = 15,000

Squaring the Circle

Come on, step up to the oche – it's time for a game of darts. But just how big is the target you are aiming at? (Let's forget about the bullseye, you'll never hit that!) We've already worked out how to calculate the distance around a circle (see pages 48–49), so now it's time to find out how to work out its area.

Let's Work It Out!

A dartboard has a radius of 22.86cm (9in) and the bullseye in the centre has a radius of 1.27cm (½in). What is the area of the dartboard outside the bullseye.

The formula for the area of circle is:

$$Area = \pi r^2$$

The radius is the distance from the centre of the circle to the edge and is half the length of the diameter.

So to calculate the area of the larger circle we have:

$$\pi r^2 =$$
$$\pi \times (22.86cm/9in)^2 =$$
$$\pi \times 522.58cm (81in) =$$
$$1,641.73cm^2 (254\tfrac{1}{2} sq. in)$$

The Maths

For any circle its circumference divided by its diameter is equal to 3.141592 … This relationship has been known since antiquity, but the Greek letter π (*pi*) was first used to describe it by Welsh mathematician William Jones (1675–1749) in 1706.

π is an irrational number and cannot be written as a fraction. Expressed as a decimal π has an infinite number of digits with no apparent pattern, although mathematicians have sought to find one by calculating π to more and more decimal places – it has now been calculated to over ten trillion (10^{13}) digits.

And for the smaller circle:

$$\pi r^2 =$$
$$\pi \times 1.27\text{cm } (\tfrac{1}{2}\text{in})^2 =$$
$$\pi \times 1.61\text{cm } (\tfrac{1}{4}\text{in}) =$$
$$5.06\text{cm}^2 \ (\tfrac{4}{5} \text{ sq. in})$$

To work out the area of the board outside the bullseye we need to subtract the area of the smaller circle from the larger one.

A Golden Photograph

The Golden Ratio created by Fibonacci's sequence of numbers (see pages 82–83), gives us a neat way to take better photographs by helping us with composition. So whether your camera is disposable, long lens or simply on your phone, get clicking – but make sure you remember the golden rule.

The Golden Ratio applied to a rectangle

The Maths

The Golden Ratio is a relationship found in both mathematics and the arts where for two numbers the ratio of the sum of the numbers to the larger number is equal to the ratio of the larger number to the smaller one.

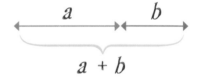

a + b is to a as a is to b

It is represented by the Greek letter φ (*phi*) and its value is 1.618033 … The ratio's application in the world outside mathematics, in design, art, architecture, music and nature, has ensured its popularity.

THE GOLDEN RULE

The Answer

So when you are taking a picture, imagine placing a Fibonacci spiral on top of the image. Then, position the most important element of your shot, e.g. someone's eyes, an important building, not at the exact centre of the image, but at the eye of the Fibonacci spiral, which is slightly off-centre. Try it – it really works!

Let's Work It Out!

Ancient Greek mathematicians first studied what we now know as the Golden Ratio because of its appearance in geometry relating to pentagons and pentagrams. In 1202, Fibonacci published his sequence of numbers (see pages 82–83), and it became apparent that the further up the sequence you move, the ratio between the numbers becomes closer and closer to the Golden Ratio.

But what does this have to do with taking photographs? If you apply the idea of the Golden Ratio to a rectangle, then the most aesthetically pleasing shape is one where the ratio of the shorter to the longer sides is somewhere around 1.6 – the value of φ. And, if you divide this rectangle again by creating a square and another rectangle, the smaller rectangle will be another golden rectangle. If you carry on, this will create a spiral shape that relates to shells seen in nature that exhibit the properties of the Fibonacci sequence.

Did You Know?

Almost 2,500 years ago, a Greek sculptor and architect called Phidias is thought to have used the Golden Ratio to design the statues he sculpted for the Parthenon, and the word 'phi' in his name actually inspired the naming of this number in the 20th century.

Mine Is Bigger Than Yours

Maths does not always involve absolute values. Sometimes we compare something to something else and determine their value relative to one another: Peter ran faster than John; Emma's hair is shorter than Jane's etc. These are known as inequalities. They also have their own symbols, which is good because that makes us look clever.

Did You Know? 12 + 3 - 4 + 5 + 67 + 8 + 9 = 100

'Medicine makes people ill, mathematics make them sad and theology makes them sinful.'
Martin Luther, German theologian

Let's Work It Out!

When you go to the cinema, all movies are given a classification that tells you whether or not it is suitable for your age group. Let's say a movie is classified '15', which means that no one younger than 15 is allowed to watch it, how would you write that as an inequality? You may also be thinking 'That's not fair!' but that's not the sort of inequality we're talking about right now.

So to watch a movie rated '15' you have to be 15 or older. So in terms of inequalities this means you need to be:

> 15

But you can also be equal to 15 ...

The Maths

We use the term inequalities to describe things that are not equal. The two most common inequalities are:

> Greater than

< Less than

Remember the narrow end always points towards the smaller number: BIG > small.

Inequalities can also include 'equals':

≥ Greater than or equal to

≤ Less than or equal to

... which means that to watch a movie rated '15' your age must be:

≥15

> **The Answer**

Let's Factor That In

Factoring a number in maths is a bit like putting it through a mincer: you use it to find out which numbers divide into it exactly, including the number 1 and the number itself. It also helps us find out which numbers other numbers have in common.

What occurs once in every minute, twice in every moment and yet never in a thousand years? (For the answer see page 112.)

Did You Know?

Let's Work It Out!
I've got 80 lollipops but I don't know if I've got 12 or 20 children coming to the party. I don't want to have to worry about dividing them up later, so how can I divide the lollipops so the children get the highest number possible in either case?

1, 2, 3, 4, 6 and 12

The factors of 12 are:

The factors of 20 are:

1, 2, 4, 5, 10 and 20

The Maths

Here we are calculating what is called the Highest Common Factor of 12 and 20. The Highest Common Factor (HCF) of two whole numbers is the largest whole number that is a factor of both.

We can also find the HCF by multiplying all the prime factors that appear in *both* lists, which in this case is just the number two, so:

$$2 \times 2 = 4$$

Another common operation involving factors is to find the Lowest Common Multiple. The Lowest Common Multiple (LCM) of two whole numbers is the smallest whole number that is a multiple of both. You work this out by multiplying all the prime factors that appear in **either** list:

$$12 = 2 \times 2 \times 3$$
$$20 = 2 \times 2 \times 5$$
$$LCM = 2 \times 3 \times 5 = 60$$

THE X FACTOR

The Answer

You can see here that the number four appears in both lists, and is the highest number that is common to both, so if I put four lollipops into each bag then whether the party is crowded or not, each child will get the same sugar rush.

Six of One and Half a Dozen of the Other

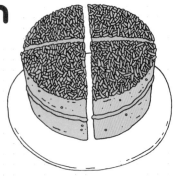

Fractions are all very well, but what do we do with them? I know I would like half of that cake, a third of that one, and that other one looks nice too, but I should probably only have a quarter. What on Earth does that add up to? I already know the answer is 'Too much'!

Let's Work It Out!

What is ½ + ⅓ + ¼?

There are three steps to adding fractions:

Step 1 Make sure the numbers on the bottom (the denominators) are the same.

Step 2 Add the top numbers (the numerators) over the denominators.

Step 3 Simplify the fraction if necessary.

Here the denominators are different so we need to make them the same. One way to do this is to find the Lowest Common Multiple (LCM) of the three numbers (see pages 96–97). The prime factors of 2, 3 and 4 multiplied together would be:

$$LCM = 2 \times 2 \times 3 = 12$$

This means our Lowest Common Denominator needs to be expressed in twelfths, so we get:

$^6/_{12}$ (equal to $^1/_2$) + $^4/_{12}$ (equal to $^1/_3$) + $^3/_{12}$ (equal to $^1/_4$)

To find the total we need to add the numerators together.

The Maths

Subtracting fractions is done in the same way, but multiplication and division are different. To multiply fractions you do this:

1. Multiply the numerators.
2. Multiply the denominators.
3. Simplify the fraction if necessary.

And to divide them, you do this:

1. Turn the second fraction upside-down.
2. Multiply the first fraction by the second fraction.
3. Simplify the fraction if necessary.

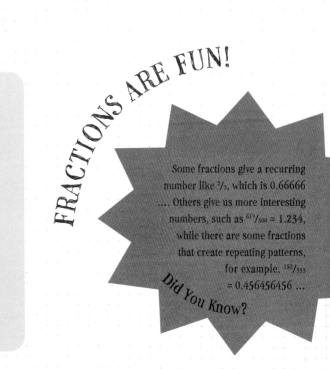

FRACTIONS ARE FUN!

Some fractions give a recurring number like $^2/_3$, which is 0.66666 .... Others give us more interesting numbers, such as $^{617}/_{500}$ = 1.234, while there are some fractions that create repeating patterns, for example, $^{152}/_{333}$ = 0.456456456 ...

Did You Know?

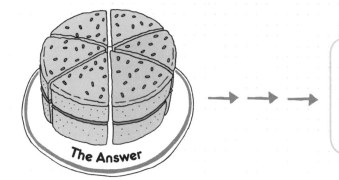

The Answer

$$^6/_{12} + {}^4/_{12} + {}^3/_{12} = {}^{13}/_{12} = 1^1/_{12}$$

$^{13}/_{12}$ is actually an improper fraction (the numerator is greater than the denominator), so definitely too much cake!

Euclidean Efficiency

Active in the late 4th century BC, Euclid was a Greek mathematician famous for his *Elements*, one of the most influential works in the history of mathematics. Very little is known about his life but his methods formed the basis of maths textbooks until the early 20th century. Among his numerous legacies was an algorithm for calculating the Highest Common Factor (HCF, see pages 96–97), without even using factors.

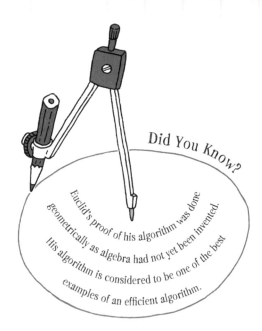

Did You Know?

Euclid's proof of his algorithm was done geometrically as algebra had not yet been invented. His algorithm is considered to be one of the best examples of an efficient algorithm.

Let's Work It Out!

What is the HCF of 36 and 15 using Euclid's Algorithm?

In Book VII of *Elements* Euclid described how to work out the HCF without listing its factors. To find the HCF of 36 and 15 carry out the following steps:

Step 1 Divide the greater number by the smaller number:

$$36 \div 15 = 2 \text{ (remainder 6)}$$

Step 2 Divide the smaller number by the remainder:

$$15 \div 6 = 2 \text{ (remainder 3)}$$

Step 3 Divide the first remainder by the second remainder:

$$6 \div 3 = 2 \text{ (remainder 0)}$$

THINK OF AN ALGORITHM AS A MATHS RECIPE!

The Answer
The last non-zero remainder is the HCF, so therefore:
HCF = 3

The Maths
An algorithm is a step-by-step process for a particular operation – a bit like a maths recipe. Another way of expressing the algorithm is like this:

For two numbers a and b:
$a \div b$ gives a remainder of r
$b \div r$ gives a remainder of s
$r \div s$ gives a remainder of t
...
$w \div x$ gives a remainder of y
$x \div y$ gives no remainder

Here y is the HCF of a and b. If the first step had produced no remainder, then b (the smaller of the two numbers) is the HCF.

Cracking the Code

Everyone loves a spy story, but being a spy is not about guns and gadgets, it is about secrets. Codes, like the substitution cipher seen here, have been used for as long as language has been written down to protect information from our enemies, famous examples being Julius Caesar, Mary Queen of Scots, and the German Enigma code during the Second World War.

Let's Work It Out!

Codes and ciphers are forms of secret communication. A code replaces entire words, phrases, or sentences with groups of letters or numbers; a cipher rearranges letters or substitutes them with other letters or symbols to disguise the message. This is called encryption or enciphering.

Here is a message you might leave for someone in your family or a friend, but what does it say?

WKH NHB LV XQGHU WKH PDW

When Julius Caesar sent coded messages to his generals his cipher used letters that were three places further along in the alphabet: so for A he used D, for E he used H, and so on. So using the key below, can you crack the code?

A	B	C	D	E	F	G	H	I	J	K	L	M	N	O	P	Q	R	S	T	U	V	W	X	Y	Z
0	1	2	3	4	5	6	7	8	9	10	11	12	13	14	15	16	17	18	19	20	21	22	23	24	25

The Answer
The message says:
'The key is under the mat'.

The Maths

To create the cipher we are adding three to our starting number, so for A this would be:

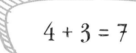

$$0 + 3 = 3$$

The number 3 represents the letter D in our cipher so we would substitute that for the letter A. E would be:

$$4 + 3 = 7$$

Here the number 7 is H, so E would become H when we were encrypting our message. When we are decoding the messages we are doing the opposite, so in this example, encryption is addition while decryption is subtraction. Using the terms of cryptology, the method used to create the code is known as the algorithm, while the table above, which is used to allow the original message (or plaintext) to be enciphered and deciphered, is known as the key.

In fact, if you look at the original encrypted message above, H is the letter that appears most often, followed closely by W. This is because E and T are the two most common letters in the alphabet, and this use of frequency analysis is one method code breakers use to crack codes.

Did You Know?

The Enigma machine was first invented in 1918 by Arthur Scherbius, a German businessman, who sold it commercially to banks. A military version of the machine was used by Nazi Germany before and during the Second World War. The Germans believed the code to be unbreakable, but code breakers first in Poland and later in the UK, helped by Alan Turing's early computer, the Bombe, managed to break the code and shorten the war by as much as two years.

Our Survey Says ...

You've done a survey and you want to do a really fancy presentation but what's the best way to present your information? Numbers by themselves are dull, but luckily there are many different types of graphs that enable us to show our findings in an exciting way.

Let's Work It Out!

Out of a group of 20 friends, these are the types of television shows they like best:

Entertainment	Food	Comedy	News	Sport
5	4	6	1	4

How can we show these as both a bar chart and a pie chart?

To make a bar chart you want to show how many people prefer each category of show. So you plot the number of people on the vertical axis and the types of show along the bottom.

Making a pie chart – a circular chart that uses sections of relative sizes to compare data – is a bit more complicated. First, for the group as a whole (20 people), you need to work out as a percentage how many people preferred each category.

Then you need to work out the angle of each section as a percentage of 360° (the number of degrees in a circle).

Entertainment	Food	Comedy	News	Sport
5	4	6	1	4
5/20 = 25%	4/20 = 20%	6/20 = 30%	1/20 = 5%	4/20 = 20%
25% of 360° = 90°	20% of 360° = 72°	30% of 360° = 108°	5% of 360° = 18°	20% of 360° = 72°

Now you can go ahead and divide up your circle accordingly (you'll need a protractor).

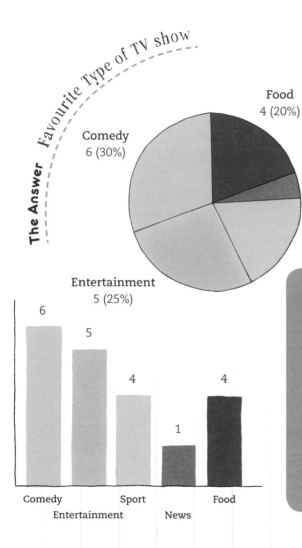

Favourite Type of TV show

Food
4 (20%)

Comedy
6 (30%)

News
1 (5%)

Sport
4 (20%)

Entertainment
5 (25%)

Tetraphobia is a fear of the number four. In China and other countries in South-east Asia, including Korea, Japan and Vietnam, the word for four sounds similar to the word for death. As a result, the number four and many other numbers containing the number four are often avoided, for example, floor numbers are skipped in buildings, and table numbers are missed out at weddings and other social occasions.

Did You Know?

The Maths

These are just two ways to show data in a graphical way, and are good for showing the relative size of data. Other types of graphs include:

Histograms: Similar to bar charts but with numbers grouped into ranges.

Line graphs: Show information that is connected in some way, e.g. change over time.

Scatter charts: Plot one set of data against another as a way to show the relationship between the two.

Pictograms: Use images to stand for a certain number of things.

105

Magic Squares

Have you ever tried Sudoku? These fiendish number puzzles are everywhere – in books, newspapers and online. Wouldn't you just love to work out how to do it? Well let's go back to basics and find out how to build magic number squares and you can take it from there.

Let's Work It Out!

How do you construct a square using consecutive numbers where every row, column and diagonal add up to the same number? Cover up the grid below, draw your own and see how you get on.

Step 1 Draw a 3 × 3 grid. Place a number 1 in the middle of the top row.

Step 2 Move through the other squares placing the numbers consecutively. Once you have placed a number remember to move:

* The square diagonally up and to the right when you can.
* The square below if you cannot.
* If you move off one edge of the square you must re-enter on the other side.

Step 3 When you place the 2 you are moving up and to the right, but as you are moving off the edge of the square the 2 is placed in the bottom right-hand corner. Likewise with the number 3 you are moving off the right-hand side of the square, so you must re-enter in the middle row on the left-hand side. The space for the 4 is occupied so it must be placed down below the three, and so on …

The Answer

8	1	6
3	5	7
4	9	2

As you can see each row, column and diagonal add up to 15. Can you do the same for a 5 × 5 grid? (For the answer see page 112.)

The Maths

The method used to construct this square is an algorithm, or a series of steps, known by many names including de la Loubère's algorithm, the staircase method and the Siamese method. Simon de la Loubère was a French mathematician and diplomat who brought back the method following his time spent in Siam (now Thailand) in the 17th century. He published his findings in a book, *A New Historical Relation to the Kingdom of Siam*, in 1693.

The method involves a simple arithmetic progression and works when you start with any odd number. (A normal magic square starts with the number one; a magic square can start with any positive number.) There is no algorithm for generating magic squares starting with an even number.

		6			9	2		
	8			6			7	
4			5					8
		2	7					3
	3			5			9	
1					3	5		
7					1			4
	6			2			1	
		4	9		8			

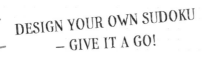

DESIGN YOUR OWN SUDOKU – GIVE IT A GO!

Did You Know?

Given any magic square, rotating it or reflecting it will produce another magic square. Not counting these as distinct, it is known that for 3 x 3 squares there is only one normal magic square, and for 4 x 4 squares there are 880 normal magic squares. As the size of the square increases the number of normal magic squares increases dramatically, and for 5 x 5 squares there are over 13 million normal magic squares!

Mind Your 'X's and 'Y's

Simultaneous equations, or equations that involve two or more unknowns that have the same value in each equation, can be infuriating but they can come in handy. So don't get too cross, and look at those 'Y's with no fear in your eyes.

Let's Work It Out!

You've been to a café with two groups of friends and you know what the bill came to each time and who had what, but what does everything cost?

The first time you went there were six of you, six of you had the set meal, five of you had coffee, and the bill came to £37.50. The second time you went there were four people, again you all had the set meal and this time only two of you had coffee, and the bill was £23. How much does the set meal and the coffee cost? So where x denotes set meals and y denotes coffees, this gives us the equation:

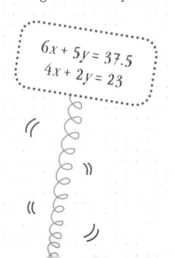

$$6x + 5y = 37.5$$
$$4x + 2y = 23$$

As none of the unknowns cancel one another out (i.e. there is not a '+ x' in one equation and a '- x' in the other) the first thing to do is to give one of the unknowns the same value in each equation. So let's do that for y:

Multiply the first equation by two to give us:
$12x + 10y = 75$

Multiply the second equation by five to give us:
$20x + 10y = 115$

The Answer

To find a value for x, subtract the first equation from the second equation to cancel out the y:

$$(20x - 12x) + (10y - 10y) = 115 - 75$$
$$8x = 40$$
$$x = 5$$

Now substitute the value for x back into the first equation and rearrange it to give us a value for y (you can check your answer by making sure it works for the other equation too):

$$6 (5) + 5y = 37.5$$
$$30 + 5y = 37.5$$
$$5y = 37.5 - 30$$
$$5y = 7.5$$
$$y = 7.5 \div 5 = 1.5$$

So the set meals cost £5 while the coffees are £1.50.

SIMULTANEOUS EQUATIONS CAN COME IN HANDY

Lunch Menu

Coffee

Set Meal

What is the total?

The Maths

Simultaneous equations require detective work: first, get one of the suspects on its own and try and get it to give up its accomplices. Use your Lowest Common Multiple (see pages 96–97) to get everyone to tell the same story, and then take one away from the other and rearrange to get the answer you want. Job done.

A Mirror Image

We see symmetry in the shapes and objects all around us.
Even our earliest art creation was a perfect example –
remember those butterfly pictures you made when you
were young? The ones where you painted on one side
of the paper and then folded it in half so the paint was
transferred to the other side? I bet you didn't realize
that was as much about maths as it was about art.

Symmetry is everywhere you look!

Did You Know?
Narcissus was a hunter in Greek mythology,
who was renowned for his beauty and
arrogance. The goddess Nemesis (you can
probably guess where this is going) lured
Narcissus to a pool where he saw his own
reflection in the water and fell in love with
it. Unable to tear himself away from his
reflection he died, and the term 'narcissist'
is now used to described people who are
fixated with themselves.

The Answer
So what about the lines of symmetry in a circle?
A line drawn at any angle that goes through the centre is
a line of symmetry, so a circle has infinite lines of symmetry.

Let's Work It Out!

So you folded your paper to make your butterfly, which makes one line of symmetry. But what about other shapes? How many lines of symmetry does a circle have?

For a shape to be symmetrical, when you fold that shape in half, the folded part must sit perfectly on top with all edges matching. But some shapes have more lines of symmetry than others.

A rectangle has two lines of symmetry

A square has four lines of symmetry:

An equilateral triangle (where all sides are the same length) has three lines of symmetry:

As you might expect, other regular polygons, also with sides of the same length have as many lines of symmetry as they have sides (try it, it's true).

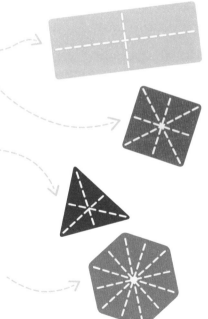

The Maths

In maths the movement of shapes is known as Transformation. There are three main transformations.

- **Reflection** The example here concerns reflection, where every point is the same distance from a central line, and the reflection has the same size as the original image.

- **Rotation** Where an image is rotated around a central point and repeated; the number of times it is repeated is known as an order. In point symmetry an image is repeated the same distance from the origin but in the opposite direction.

- **Translation** Where each point of a shape or object is moved the same distance in the same direction.

pp.38–39 I Want to be Alone
$x = 10$, $x = 8$, $x = 6$, $x = 4$, $x = 7$

pp.40–41 How Fast Is He Running?
37.58km (23.35 miles) per hour

pp.80–81 Helpful Hints for Multiplying
1. 36 **6.** 144
2. 88 **7.** 54
3. 24 **8.** 132
4. 84 **9.** 48
5. 70 **10.** 162

pp.88–89 The 'I's Have It!
The word is 'FIVE'.
Take away 'F' and 'E', and you get 'IV' (the Roman numeral for four). Take away 'I' and you are left with 'V' (the Roman numeral for five).

pp.96–97 Let's Factor That In
The letter 'm'.

pp.106–107 Magic Squares

17	24	1	8	15
23	5	7	14	16
4	6	13	20	22
10	12	19	21	3
11	18	25	2	9

For this grid each row, column and diagonal add up to 65.

ANSWERS!